MourneQuest

Secret of the Silver Orb

For Karen, Jack, Tess and Grace
with special thanks to
Lindsey and Catherine

MourneQuest

Secret of the Silver Orb

Garry McElherron

Illustrations by John Farrelly
And Alan Perry

O:cellaris

First published 2012

Copyright © 2012 by Garry McElherron

The moral right of the author/illustrator has been asserted.

www.mournequest.com

ISBN 978-1-291-11511-6

Contents

"He's late. He's never late…"

Chapter 1
Waiting for Da

The jagged back of Carrick Little Mountain swept down to the small village of Springwell Port and at the far end of a long wooden pier, stood a small boy. He rocked back and forth on his heels, eyes shut tight to block out the terrifying sight of the rough seas. But the waves crashing against the pier only made him more anxious. He forced himself to think of home and of how it would feel to snuggle close to his father by the fire that evening, breathing in the smell of the sea from his clothes and watching the freckles dance on his face as he brought his tales of the fishing trip to life.

The sound of a ship's bell startled the boy and when he opened his eyes, he spied the main sail of a fishing boat rounding the head of the bay. It rode high in the water, carried on the strong tidal currents and he could tell she was doing at least seven knots. He held his breath as she passed through the treacherous reef that had claimed many a boat in its time. Then, finally, the boy's face broke into a smile.

"Da!"

From the number of herring gulls and oystercatchers circling the mast, the boy knew there had been a good catch.

His father skilfully steered the boat towards the pier.

Once he was near enough, he cupped his mouth with his hands and called, "Jack, get ready to catch the ropes!"

Jack quickly rolled up the sleeves of his grandfather shirt. He grunted as he caught and lifted the sodden ropes up and over the edge of the pier.

When the boat safely moored, Jack's father scrambled up the rickety ladder and stood in front of him, towering against the early morning sky. He was a giant of a man, just over six and a half foot tall with shoulders so broad they looked like they could carry his boat all the way home. His face was permanently red, weathered from the harsh sea winds. He scooped Jack up into his strong arms and gave him a hug so tight Jack's ribs ached.

"Da! Your jumper's itchy!" said Jack, laughing as he struggled to get free.

"What do ya mean, boy? It's never itchy! Y'know your Nanna Tess made it for me. Said she knitted it with the softest wool in all of Ireland and she even put a lucky stitch in it for me." He winked at Jack. "Hasn't let me down yet, you know."

Jack grinned. "Nanna always talks like that." He helped his father haul the baskets of mackerel and herring up from the boat but as he bent down to grab another basket, something caught his eye. He found himself staring down into an unusually smooth patch of the dark water, trying to make sense of it. The reflection staring back at him had foam-white hair and a ripple-wrinkled face. How could that be? Now he looked closer, he could see that it looked like him, but as a very old man. His stomach tightened and his throat dried up.

"What's keeping you, Jack? Old Mr. Russell will be along any minute with his horse and cart for the fish and you know how he hates to be kept waiting.'

No matter how hard he tried, Jack could not tear himself away from the face staring back at him from the water.

"Jack! *Jack!* Did you hear me?" His Da waved his hand in front of his son's face.

"Huh? Sorry Da. What'd you say?"

Jack glanced from his Da back into the water. This time it was his own face looking up at him. The knot in his stomach loosened.

"Here's our man!"

Old Mr. Russell had come to a stop right at the end of the pier. He too must have been watching out for the Fishermans' return. The stormy seas didn't bother his horse at all. The old beast was near retirement and had seen all kinds of weather. Jack and his Da loaded up the cart while the horse stood, patiently waiting.

"Here ya go, Matthew. And here's what I owe you as well."

Jack's father Matthew thanked the fishmonger and he threw the coins into the air before catching and pocketing them.

"Jack, we're rich. Come on now, I'm starvin'. I'm so hungry I could eat a horse." He leaned in closer. "Not Old

Russell's nag though. That one's a bit skinny and besides, who else'll get my fish to market?"

Jack laughed and slipped his hand into his father's. He felt the hard skin of the fisherman's palm criss-crossed with deep furrows until his fingertips came across a new bump.

"What's that Da?"

"Ach that, it's nothin', just a wee rope burn. Your Nanna Tess has the cure for it."

He grabbed Jack and lifted him high over his head onto his shoulders.

"Daaaaa!" Jack shouted. "Do you know what age I am?" And he wriggled and shook trying to get back down.

Matthew gripped Jack's ankles and leaned backwards, forcing him to hold on to even tighter.

"My Jack's never too old for this," he laughed.

Together they headed home, through fields of summer worn grass. It was calm now, for even this short distance from shore they were sheltered. They passed the great wooden spokes of the Corn Mill, gently churning the stream as the water flowed down into the sea.

Matthew pointed at the high walls. "Remind me to tell you how your Great Granda helped build that. He came from a long line of stone masons, you know?"

Jack had heard the story countless times but he never tired of it. Soon they came to a halt. Jack hitched a leg over his father's shoulder and slid down to the ground.

"It's good to be home, son!"

Matthew reached up and knocked the horseshoe on the half door for luck. He gave a quick glance back at his son and winked.

"By the way, I haven't forgotten what day it is." He pushed open the door, ducking his head as he entered.

But Jack didn't follow him inside. Not just yet. He looked up to where the curling smoke drifted from the chimney, blackening the thatch, then down to the stone walls beneath, as white as his Nanna Tess' apron.

Only the archway surrounding the front door was unpainted, made of large granite rocks. Jack walked to the doorway and stood there for a moment. His father was safely home and everything was all right. By the peat fire, darning a sock, sat his mother, Martha. The sock fall from her lap as his father drew her to her feet and hugged her. Jack glanced across to the chimney breast and down to the fire that glowed under the cast iron cauldron, its light throwing shadows over the uneven earthen tiles on the floor. Then his eyes came to rest on the dimly lit snug, where Nanna Tess sat, watching him.

Chapter 2

Dandelion Wish

Nanna Tess was over a hundred years old and she wore the seasons like the shawl on her shoulders. Her hair had long since turned from flaxen to silver, tied in a bun and fixed in place with a spike of hawthorn. When she saw Jack standing there, she gave him a wide toothless grin, but, as always, her eyes seemed full of sorrow. He often caught her staring towards the fire embers, as if she'd lost something there.

"Come in, Jack." Martha beckoned. "We've something for ya."

She tried her best to hide a small object behind her back, spinning on her brogues when Jack ran to see what she was holding.

"You're too slow!" Matthew laughed. "Now close your eyes and hold out your hand."

"Happy birthday!" said Martha as Jack's fingers closed around his present.

"See if you can guess what it is," said Matthew.

Jack kept his eyes shut. He could smell linseed oil.

"I know what it is! Can I open my eyes now?"

"Go on."

In the palm of Jack's hand sat a tiny boat. "It's

exactly the same as yours, Da."

"It should be. I whittled it from the top part of my boat's mast, so she'll still hold up in a gale."

Jack studied it closely. "It's perfect. It even has the name, the *Caisear Bhan* on the stern and look, a tiny fisherman at the helm."

"That's supposed to me Jack. Riding the waves!"

Jack noticed a tiny circular mark. Had it been etched onto the bow? Or was it just a mark on the wood? There was nothing similar on his father's boat.

"I sewed the sails," said Martha.

"Thanks Ma! Thanks Da!"

Jack ran to his Nanna and sat the boat on her apron. "Look Nanna! Isn't it the best present ever?"

"It's wonderful Jack." She examined it carefully, before handing the boat back. Then she leant on her stick and slowly rose to her feet.

"Come with me, I've something for ya too." Leaning on her grandson's shoulder for support, she walked slowly outside and together they sat themselves down on the front step.

"You know Jack, you're ten now, nearly the man of the house."

Jack had never thought of himself that way before.

"But there's a few things I need to tell ya. Your Ma and Da love you dearly, and you know why they made you the boat, don't you? They hope it'll stop you fretting so much when your Da's out at sea."

"I know Nanna, but..."

"But nothing, Jack. Your Da has no choice, fishing's all Matthew knows. I know your Ma fusses over you so, but that's only to be expected given that she nearly lost you all those years ago."

A wave of sadness swept over Jack. They almost never spoke about that time.

"And I know you'd love to go out fishing with your Da, and I promise you one day you will."

"But you know how scared I am, Nanna."

"I know, but you must stop being so hard on yourself Jack. You couldn't have changed things. Nobody could have changed what happened that day."

"But if only..."

"Now you listen to me Jack. What happened wasn't your fault. It was no one's fault. And I'll keep telling you that until you believe me. But now is not the time or place to dwell on such things. It's your special day, and I took you out here to show you the most wonderful thing you'll ever see."

"What's that?"

The old lady smiled. "As a little girl I watched your Great-Great Granda Liam, Matthew's Great-Granda, build this cottage." She pointed to the granite round the door. "Did you know the stones in this archway came all the way from Tollymore Forest?"

"But that's miles away! Why didn't he just use the rocks in the fields like he did with the rest of the cottage? They're lying all over the place."

"I asked him that very same question Jack, and do

ya know what he said to me?"

"No. What?"

"You'll see," she replied, reaching down. She pulled some clumps of grass out of the dirt beside a stone at the foot of the archway. Jack noticed for the first time that there was a celtic rope design carved on the stone. He must have been through the archway thousands of times and this was the first he knew of the carving. Tess gently put her hand in behind the stone and moved it to one side.

"See *what*?" he asked.

"That's all Liam said -'you'll see'. Now look." She lifted out a battered wooden box. "Here you go," she said, handing it to him.

"For me?" said Jack. He brushed away some of the dust, revealing a circular carving on the lid.

"Well who else would it be for?"

"Has this box been here all this time? Sure I didn't even know the archway had that loose stone."

"There's lots of things ya don't know about this archway Jack. But there's plenty of time for that. Now are ya not dying to know what's inside o' the bloomin' box?"

"Of course I am, Nanna." He went to open it but suddenly Nanna Tess' hand slammed down on the lid. Jack jumped but Nanna didn't seem to notice the fright she had given him.

"There's a tale of a birthday, just like yours, a summer solstice birthday, one of equal day and night. It makes it very special, you know?"

Jack didn't know, but he didn't feel he could ask

either. Nanna removed her hand and nodded at him. Carefully, Jack lifted the lid. The faint scent of wild roses escaped from within. The box was full of dried petals.

"Look properly," said Nanna and he began to pick through them until he found... a dandelion, fluffy and white and with all its seed heads ready to let fly.

Jack's heart sank. But he didn't want Nanna to see that he was disappointed.

"Thanks, Nanna," he said, forcing a smile.

She leaned in close to his ear. "Don't be disappointed Jack."

"I'm not Nanna, honestly."

"It's not just any old dandelion, ya know," she whispered, flicking the tip of his nose with her finger. "It's special too." She snapped her fingers close to Jack's face, making him blink. When he looked again she was holding a tiny piece of parchment in her long wrinkled fingers.

"Where'd that come from?"

"Never mind. Don't ya want to know what's written on it?"

Jack's heart was thumping. "Yes."

"The words on this page hold the greatest secret of all, Jack. They hold the way to a whole new world."

Jack's eyes shone with excitement.

"Ready?"

Jack nodded. As ready as he was ever likely to be.

"Tongue be rolled,
Eyes do lock,
Silent wish told,
Silver orb freed of clock."

For a moment after she'd finished reading, Nanna became totally still. Then, without any warning she snatched the parchment back and stuffed it into the pocket of her apron.

"But what does it mean, Nanna?"

Instead of answering, she stuck out her tongue at him, and then curled the edges upwards, holding it in place with her puckered lips.

Jack laughed and tried to copy her. "Di dan't do it," he said, his fat tongue sticking out of his mouth.

"Try again."

After the third go, he managed to roll his tongue as she had.

"You've got it!' Nanna was delighted. "Now make your wish." Nanna Tess closed her eyes so Jack did the same.

"I wish I could fly... no wait... be big... no wait... be strong... no..."

"All right Jack, calm down," said Nanna Tess, chuckling. "Remember this. The wish must be made in silence, *inside* your head, never out loud. Do you understand?"

"Yes Nanna, in my head, never out loud."

"And Jack, after you've wished, you must blow through your rolled tongue. Not a single clock can be left behind."

He nodded, but he was puzzled.
"Nanna?"
"Yes ?"
"What's a clock?"
Nanna Tess smiled. "They're the tiny seed heads on

a dandelion. Some people call them sprigs, others call them clocks. Look." She fixed him with her watery blue eyes.

"Now you heed me Jack. The most important thing about a dandelion wish is that it must be pure of heart. Ya can't go wishing harm on anyone or making someone love you 'cos if you do... Well, no matter ... Oh... and another thing, your wish can only be made on your birthday."

"Like today."

"Why else do ya think I gave you the box?" Nanna Tess struggled to get up from the step. She leant heavily on her stick and waved away Jack's help. "I'm goin' in."

Jack watched as she hobbled back indoors. He was left alone.

That night Jack lay in his bed, too warm to sleep, thinking about what Nanna Tess had said. He practiced curling up his tongue, just as she had. Restless, he hung over the edge of his bed and from underneath, slid out the battered box. His fingers felt their way around the strange circular carving on the lid. He counted five indentations at the edge of the circle. They seemed to move slightly when he pressed them.

Inside, the dandelion lay undisturbed amongst the petals. When he touched it, a strange tingle, almost like a nettle sting, ran through his fingertips. Was he ready to make his special birthday wish? He padded across the room, cradling the dandelion in one hand, and swung open his bedroom window. The cool air made the clocks shiver very slightly. Carefully, Jack held the dandelion up to the night sky. The stars were as bright as he'd ever seen them.

Sure, no one's looking, he thought.

He took a deep breath, and then rolled his tongue the way Nanna Tess had shown him, closed his eyes, and made his wish. He had thought hard about what it should be, and now he was sure.

"I wish it would snow on my house tomorrow!"

Then he blew as hard as he could.

The clocks billowed up and danced in a circle just above his head before the summer breeze sucked them out through the window into the night sky. He watched as they floated away, then placed the bare stalk back in the box and slid it under his bed again. Where did the dandelion clocks go when they blew away? Would his crazy wish come true? With this thought, he finally drifted off to sleep.

Next morning Jack's breath formed in a cold cloud above his head. He shivered and pulled the patchwork quilt tight around him. How could it feel so cold in June? He glanced towards his window, where the brown linen curtains flapped lazily in the breeze. Then, dozens of dandelion clocks flitted through the window into his room and he remembered his wish of the previous evening.

No... Jack sat bolt upright in his bed. These weren't clocks.

These were snowflakes.

He jumped out of bed, ran to the window, and leaned out. Something icy cold slipped down the collar of his nightshirt, startling him. He looked up, rubbing the back of his neck, and stared in disbelief at the melting icicles dripping onto the sill.

Icicles... in summer? Jack laughed.

The glare from the sun was so bright that he had to

shield his eyes. But Jack forced himself to look outside.

"It came true! It came true! My wish came true!"

Jack pulled the window open and leapt out, landing headfirst into a deep bank of snow. He was beside himself.

He rolled neat little snowballs and threw them at a Meadow Pipit and Grey Wagtail perched on the nearby fence. He watched the birds take flight towards the green fields... *green* fields! So it had only snowed on the cottage, nowhere else.

Jack ran round in circles, howling with laughter. The snow was melting quickly now, but the more he thought of what had happened the more he laughed. It was ridiculous! Snow in June – and all because of the magic dandelion and his special wish! Or was he dreaming?

Suddenly, out of the corner of his eye Jack was aware of a dark shape flashing across the hillside.

Seconds later he saw it again - something huge and unnatural, traveling at great speed across the hedgerows.

An icy chill ran down his spine. He wasn't laughing now.

"Jack, where are ye?" Martha shouted from the breakfast table.

"I'm here, Ma. Outside." Jack was standing in his nightshirt.

Martha put her hand on her hips. Honestly, that lad hadn't the sense he was born with! "Your breakfast's on the table and it's not gonna eat itself! Now get in here!" She wiped her hands on a dishcloth expecting Jack any second. By the time she'd eaten a second slice of soda bread, there was still no sign of him. Tutting, she went to the window, pushing it open. There he was, standing looking a little dazed in the morning dew. The strong summer sun had melted all the snow.

"What on earth are you up to?"

"Nothin' Ma." He looked as if he was in a world of his own.

"It doesn't look like nothin' to me. You'll catch your death running about in your nightshirt. What are you doing out this early anyway?"

Jack seemed to snap out of his trance. He turned and beamed at her. "Sure if I told ya, you wouldn't believe me anyway."

Chapter 3

The Storm

Late summer turned to autumn, followed by winter storms, which sometimes meant that Matthew stayed on shore, at home with the family. Jack loved his Da to be home, but he knew that no fishing meant no wages. Spring released Matthew from winter's imprisonment, made the fishing more reliable, and Martha relaxed, knowing there would be plenty of food on the table once again. But throughout that year, all Jack could think about was his next wish. He punched the air when the first of the swallows returned.

It was summer again. He would soon turn eleven.

Under Nanna Tess' watchful eye, Jack picked the first ripe dandelion he saw in the garden and put it in his box waiting for his birthday. It couldn't come quickly enough. "Let's see what wish you choose this year, lad," Nanna said. "You're a whole year older, so y'are."

The day before his birthday, Jack pulled on his boots. It was barely light and his father was already ambling down the hill towards the pier whistling *Fiddler's Green* as he always did when he was about to go off to sea. His navy reefer jacket slung over his shoulder on a hooked index finger.

"Wait for me!" Jack shouted. He raced off and jumped onto his father's back.

"Whoa, aren't ya getting a bit too old for that?" Matthew made a play of staggering under Jack's weight.

"Never Da, remember?"

"I remember. It's me that must be gettin' too old," Matthew laughed.

Jack hopped down and they walked side by side.

"You look freezing. The tip of your nose is pure red."

"I'm fine Da, honest."

"I shouldn't have rushed you. Look at you. You're only half dressed." Matthew took his jumper off, pulled it over Jack's head, and fed his arms through the armholes. "There, that's better. Sure it nearly fits ya."

The huge jumper hung lopsided off Jack's shoulder and the sleeves dangled way beyond his wrists.

"I can't even see me fingers."

Matthew bent to fold the sleeves back so Jack's hands were visible again. "There, sure that's better," he said, pulling on his jacket.

They reached the pier and watched the summer sun creeping over the earth's curved rim, turning the calm Irish Sea golden.

Matthew smiled. "Perfect day for fishing!"

"Yeah, hope so." Jack could not understand his father's love of the sea. He watched him checking the boat over, rewinding ropes, and unfurling sails ready for the voyage ahead. Matthew was totally at ease, happy to be back on board. Once he was sure all was as it should be, he jumped back onto the pier, bent down and kissed Jack on the forehead.

"You'll be back on time, won't you Da?"

Matthew ruffled the boy's curls with his huge hand. "Now don't you go worrying yourself. I'll be back at the usual time in the morning. I know what tomorrow is and I wouldn't miss it for the world."

Jack watched the *Caisear Bhan* leave the dock. He held up his little boat, closed one eye, and squinted with the other until the boat in his palm and the one out at sea became the same size. For a while, they seemed to sail side by side before his father's vessel grew smaller and smaller.

Suddenly, the screech of a seagull startled Jack and he dropped the little boat. It hit the cobbles and the tiny mast snapped in two. Jack crouched to pick up the pieces and looked at them in disbelief. His precious boat... How could he have been so careless? He stood up, looking out to sea. He scratched at an itch on his neck. The jumper... No! He roared after his father, "Da, Da, you gotta come back...you forgot your jumper... your lucky jumper Da! Nanna's lucky stitch...!"

But there was no sign of Matthew's boat. With a piece of the broken boat in each hand, Jack trudged home. There was a hard knot at the top of his tummy. Once he was home, he took off the jumper, hung it on the hook in the porch, and went to his room. Slumped on his bed, Jack tried to re-join the splintered edges of the mast, but as soon as he let them go, they fell apart.

His Da would know how to mend it, but Jack didn't want him to know what had happened to the little boat. He ducked his head under the bed and lifted out the battered box. Inside lay the fresh new dandelion, and beside it lay the dried up stalk from the previous year. Carefully he sat the pieces of the boat beside them and closed the lid.

Jack lay on his back, still holding the box, and stared up at the rafters. In the centre of an elaborate spider's web a trapped fly fought for freedom, and at the edge, the spider perched motionless, watching it struggle. Jack couldn't bear it. He set the box down and reached behind the headboard for his hurley stick. Leaping up from the bed, he swung wildly for the web, bringing it down along with a great lump of plaster. The spider scuttled across the ceiling into a dark corner.

"What's going on in there?" Martha shouted.

"Nothing, Ma!"

"That's a mighty noisy nothing," she replied. "Your breakfast is waiting and your chores won't do themselves. Get a move on."

Jack busied himself for the rest of day, but he couldn't stop thinking of the fly trapped in the web. And of his boat with its broken mast. The hard knot was still there in his tummy when he went to bed that night, and it took a while before he slept.

It was a roar of thunder that woke him in the early hours of the next morning. Seconds later an explosion of light filled his room, swiftly followed by another crack of thunder. Jack dashed to his window. Dark clouds clashed as another whip of lightning ripped through the cloudburst. Jack counted slowly as Nanna Tess had taught him. "One, two three..." He reached ten before the next explosion of thunder splintered the air.

"Da...!" Jack ran from his room and into to the porch, nearly crashing into his mother.

"Jack, it's a summer storm, that's all," she told him.

"It's my fault Ma. It's all my fault." He grabbed his

father's Aran jumper from the porch.

"What is? Jack, what's your fault?" Martha tried to pull him towards her but Jack wriggled free.

"His lucky jumper. He's not wearing it. He gave it to me 'cos I was cold. It's his lucky jumper, though, Ma. With the lucky stitch that Nanna made for him. He's not safe now and it's my fault. What if the sea..."

"Calm down Jack!" Martha led him firmly back to his room. Lifting his quilt over their heads, she wrapped them both inside. Jack lay in his mother's arms listening to the calming rhythm of her heartbeat. It drowned out the chaos of the storm and although he fought it, he finally fell asleep, still clutching the jumper.

Chapter 4

Lost

When Jack awoke the next morning, he ran straight to the porch and pulled open the cottage door. The scene outside was one of devastation. Uprooted trees, ripped from the earth, lay like thrown-away playthings. Overflowing streams from the hill behind the cottage gushed through the dry stone walls that lined the fields. Jack had never seen anything like it. Clutching his father's jumper, he bolted down the garden path and through the gap in the wall where the gate hung off its hinges.

Martha raced after him. "Get back here!" she roared.

But this time Jack ignored her as he raced down to the pier. He stared out across the waters, which were calm now, and a muddy brown colour. He stood for what seemed like hours. There was no sign of the *Caisear Bhan*. Suddenly he could fend off the fear no longer. Great tears welled up in his eyes and he began to sob. His breaths came short and fast and he slumped down onto the wooden pier as his mother arrived.

Breathless, Martha crouched down and put her arms around him. "It's alright Jack, it's alright."

"He's late, Ma... He's never late."

"Now you know that's not true Jack. There's plenty of times when he comes in a bit late. Come on, son, he'll be back soon." She stroked his cheek, scanning the empty horizon. "Jack, you're freezing."

"I don't care."

"Well I do," said Martha, her voice soft but strong. "And I know your Da too. He'll be riding out the storm well beyond the headland, safe and sound, and he'll arrive all full of himself and his adventures before lunchtime. You don't want him to think you've been worrying about him, do ya?"

Jack shook his head.

"No, of course you don't. Now will you not at least come home for something to eat? You can come back and wait for him after, I promise."

"Swear?"

Martha took Jack's face in her hands. "Yes I swear." She took off her shawl and wrapped it tightly round his shoulders. One hand found its way through the folds of cloth and into hers. The other still held the jumper. Martha threw a last anxious look out to sea. "Let's go," she said.

Back at the cottage, they found Nanna Tess standing in the doorway with Old Mr. Russell.

"You'd best go in, Martha," she said quietly. "Jack, you stay out here with me." She tried to get him to help her clear up some of the storm damage but Jack strained to hear the voices from inside. What was going on? He could tell by the deep tones that Old Mr. Russell spoke for a long long time. Then there was silence.

A few moments later, a painful scream tore through the air.

Jack ran to the door and barged inside. His mother was bent forward in her chair, her face buried in her hands.

"What's wrong Ma… what's wrong?"

She looked up, her eyes dark.

"Tell me!"

"They…" Her voice cracked and she stretched a hand out to him. "They found your father's boat this morning. Crashed against the rocks."

"And…?" Jack could hardly breathe.

"He…, he wasn't on board …"

The silence that followed was deafening and a pain stabbed at Jack's heart like the life was spilling from it. It couldn't be happening, it just couldn't. Today was his day, his special day… his eleventh birthday. His Da had promised…

He grabbed his father's jumper and ran to his bedroom, slamming the door behind him. Nanna Tess knocked, offering lunch, but Jack ignored her. When she opened the door, he pretended to be asleep. But his mind wheeled and circled, aching to find a solution. He had never felt so fearful.

He stared at the jumper - where was the lucky stitch of which Nanna had boasted? *Where*? If only his Da hadn't insisted that he put it on yesterday morning. But as the evening light softened the room, Jack's mind turned to what was hidden under his bed. Perhaps he could do something. From under his bed he dragged out the battered wooden box and threw its lid open. Inside lay the fresh dandelion he'd picked a few days before. He lifted it up, turning it between finger and thumb. He tried to believe in it, tried to believe what Nanna had told him. With this, he had the power to change the past twenty-four hours as if they'd never happened. Jack threw open the bedroom window, clutching the dandelion in his fist. His heart was thumping. He rolled his tongue, squeezed his eyes tighter than he had ever done before and made his wish. Then he blew. A torrent of clocks burst upwards and off into the evening winds. Jack watched them until they vanished from sight. He had placed every ounce of hope in his wish. His muscles ached as if he had just run a hundred miles. He climbed back into his bed, and rolled his father's jumper into a pillow. The wool smelled of Matthew and of the seaweed-shoreline and it soothed him. He closed his eyes and fell asleep.

When Jack woke, the morning sun was shining through his curtains. In his hand lay the dandelion stalk, limp and bare, its clocks gone. He put it back into the box, then pushed it under his bed and sat for a while staring at his door, daring himself to open it. Had his wish come true? Eventually he got to his feet and opened the door. The house was eerily quiet. Holding his breath, he walked across the passage to his parents' room and opened their door.

His mother was asleep on top of the bedclothes clasping a photograph to her chest. She looked tiny. Jack was used to seeing her all alone in the bed while his Da was at sea but this was different.

"Ma."

Her eyes flickered. "Is that you, Matthew?"

A lump swelled in Jack's throat. "No Ma, just me." He turned, leaving her alone, and headed outside. Settling himself on the stoop at the front door, he propped his head in his hands. Shadows crept over the garden between the flowers, drooped heavy from the storm. Hours went by but Jack did not move. He just stared straight ahead, his gaze fixed on the gap in the wall.

Martha gave up trying to get him indoors, bringing him a full plate of food at lunchtime. He gave no sign of hearing her. And he didn't eat. When she came back a little later, it hadn't been touched. "You have to eat something Jack. You'll make yourself ill. Your Da'd be cross seeing good food goin' ta waste. Please now, won't ya eat something for me?"

But Jack continued to stare down the lane, praying he would see the top of a flat cap or hear a familiar tune being whistled, but none came. He sat from first light until the sun set. But there was still no sign of his father. The ache in his stomach wasn't hunger or even fear. It was growing anger.

Just before she went to bed, Nanna Tess came to the doorway. Her candle cast a gentle honeyed glow on her ancient features.

"Jack…" she said.

He jumped to his feet, turned, and pushed his face within an inch of hers. "You!" he roared. "You're a liar… You promised me my wish would come true... Where's my Da? Where is he?"

He dashed past her to his bedroom and threw himself onto his bed pounding his fists into the mattress. Then he buried his head deep into his father's jumper and after many hours, cried himself to sleep.

Chapter 5

Nightmare

Jack woke himself screaming. His legs thrashed like snapping scissors on top of his bedclothes. In his nightmare, he had seen a spider's web, only this time it was underwater and made of fishing nets. Instead of a tiny insect struggling to break free in the centre, there was a man.

"Daaaaaaa!" He sat bolt upright, arms outstretched, clambering for the fading image at the end of his bed. "Don't go."

But his Da wasn't there. Jack grabbed the quilt, pulled it over his head and rocked back and forth, his breath rapid and shallow. A few moments later, above the beat of his own breathing there was a sound like rushing water, and soon his ears were filled with the thundering sound of the sea. Would this nightmare ever end? He squeezed his father's jumper over his ears but it didn't help.

He flung the quilt from his back and leapt to the floor. Nanna Tess' box. That was where the sounds were coming from. He grabbed it but the lid wouldn't budge. He tugged on it again and again.

"Come on ya…"

Suddenly the lid released and the box spewed its contents all over the floor. Jack gathered up the broken pieces of the boat and tucked them into his pocket. Then he lifted up the dried-up dandelion stalk, the one from his tenth birthday. For a moment he couldn't quite believe what he was seeing. There it was, glimmering like a fragile crystal… a single dandelion clock.

But my first wish did *come true,* thought Jack. *It did snow on my house.*

Carefully he touched the clock with his index finger. All of a sudden a shock spiraled through his arm, rocketing upwards. Blazing now, the single clock jerked furiously on the dandelion stalk, wrenching Jack's arm straight outward. It had the strength of ten men and it scalded into his palm. No matter how hard he tried, he couldn't shake it off.

"Let go!"

The head of the dandelion turned on its stalk. It was as if it was looking at him, defiantly.

"I said let go of me!"

The dandelion paused for a moment as if to consider Jack's outburst before turning away again, spinning and swirling frantically in the air. Jack shot across the room, and collided with the window frame. For a few seconds he lay dazed in a heap on the bedroom floor before his arm jerked into the air again as the clock on the dandelion hammered furiously on the windowpane. Then Jack heard splintering glass and when he got to his feet, he watched as crystalline webs snaked at lightning speed across the glass' surface, shattering his reflection. The dandelion exploded through the window taking half the wall and the roof down with it. Jack bounced off the sill, and ploughed through the garden before coming to rest at the door of the cottage. The clock on the dandelion pounded on the loose corner stone of the archway, the one Nanna had moved to reveal the box to Jack exactly a year earlier.

No matter how hard Jack tried, the dandelion would not let him go. He grabbed the corner stone, digging his fingernails deep into the mortar joints and pulling as hard as he could. Finally, the stone shifted and a sea of slaters, spiders, and silverfish surged over his boots. He retched as the dandelion dragged his hand through their seething swarm. At last, the solitary clock let him go and flew off, into the dark cavity behind the rock.

From inside the house Jack heard a key turn and watched as the latch lifted. The front door fell ajar. Jack lay on the ground gasping for breath, relieved that the ordeal was over at last.

Chapter 6

Transformation

After a few moments Jack realised no one was coming out. He picked himself up and took a few steps back from the cottage to get a better look at the damage. Half the wall was missing and he could see right into his bedroom. Part of the thatched roof had fallen in. How was he going to explain this? And how on earth had Ma and Nanna Tess slept through all the racket?

Jack's bloodied knees hurt. He went inside and was looking on one of the shelves for Nanna Tess' special healing ointment when the front door slammed shut behind him. Startled, he spun round.

"Who's there?"

Neither Martha nor Nanna replied.

Just the wind, Jack thought.

Something flittered across the wall in front of him but before he could work out what it was, it vanished… But seconds later, there it was again. Jack shook his head. It must be his shadow from the firelight. He was a fool for giving himself such a scare. But something made him turn to check. The fire was nearly out. Then the shadow stretched up an arm. The hairs on the back of Jack's neck stood up. The shadow raised a second arm and began to stretch up the wall and onto the thatch, creeping forward. Jack could barely breathe. It was as if the shadow was pressing down on him.

It's after me!

Despite his unsteady legs, he made a break for the front door and grabbed at the latch, pulling as hard as he could. But it wouldn't budge.

The sound of sparking wood made him turn back towards the fire and now he had to shield his eyes from the blazing wood embers. White-hot sparks seemed to hop from the grate, taking flight along the chimney breast and lighting up every darkened corner of the room.

Everywhere he looked Jack could see fragments of dust turning to starlight, and cobwebs unravelling, sending strands of thread across the rafters that then swelled up, as if they were turning back into the thick boughs of trees they had once been. On the fire, the cauldron twisted and contorted, spilling its boiling contents into the room, sizzling and hissing as it engulfed the hearth, creating a scalding river that Jack had to leap to avoid.

Jack tried to shield his eyes with his hands but to his horror, he found he could see straight through them. Now his wrists and arms were fading away. He screamed for help but no sound came. When he shut his eyes that didn't help either. His eyelids were transparent. Where was Ma? Where was Nanna Tess? Jack willed them to come and help him, but there was no sign of them as the home he loved twisted and fractured under some terrible unknown force.

He didn't know where to stand. The uneven stone walls blurred and softened becoming briefly smooth, polished, and then invisible, as the room dissolved around him. The horrifying transformation continued, with Jack frozen in the midst of it, unable to take in what was happening. In desperation he fell to the ground, making himself as small as he possibly could, hoping that this waking nightmare would end.

Jack didn't know how much time passed before more familiar sounds began to register, though they weren't sounds he connected with home. Bushes bustled, water cascaded over rock, and the earth's damp scent filled his nostrils. As he found the courage to stand up and look around, everything became solid again. But this was no longer his home. Jack found himself standing ankle deep in wet grass in the crumbling ruins of an ancient cottage. It was nighttime, and the cottage was surrounded by a thick forest. Suddenly, ear-piercing sounds made him duck and cover his head with his arms.

"Scraaaawwwwkkkkkkkk......"

His muscles tightened, his spine grew rigid, and his mouth clenched so tight he felt a tooth in the back of his jaw crack.

"Scraaaawwwwkkkkkkkk......"

The second snarling shriek was even louder. He couldn't tell what direction it was coming from but Jack didn't want to wait to find out. Despite the pain in his knees and arms, he fled, darting between trees, tumbling over twisted branches, his lungs choking for air. Tripping on a mossy stone, he cascaded headfirst down a steep ravine, sliding and twisting through cold earth, arms flailing as he tried to stop his fall, until he splashed down into an icy cold river. Instinctively, he grabbed a thin branch sticking out from the embankment and clung on to it as tightly as he could, gasping from the shock of the cold water.

The wild chilling screams continued. They seemed to gain ground with each horrific outburst.

"Who are you? I've done nothing wrong. Just leave me alone," Jack shouted. "Help me, please someone, help me!"

All of a sudden, the rushing water stopped mid-flow, as though touched by an icy hand. Small foaming bubbles began to rise, cracking and popping as they hit the surface. Jack watched them grow and grow until thirteen huge hexagonal rocks crashed up through the river's surface. As soon as they were settled, the water began to flow again, gushing between each rock to create multiple waterfalls.

He didn't have time to think how this was possible; the terrifying shrieks were catching up with him. He clambered out of the water onto the nearest rock, stumbling on its slimy green surface, his arms flying outward to balance himself. He hopped to the next stone, wobbling horribly as it tilted from side to side. One mistake and he would fall into the river's fast flowing current. The next rock dipped heavily into the water. He began to topple to one side but managed somehow to right himself. Behind him, there was a terrific splash and when he looked back, Jack could see something pale and horrid screaming and gurgling as the current swept it off downstream. The shrieking stopped for a short time. But not for long.

With massive effort, he scrambled across the rest of the rocks until he reached solid ground, falling up a set of worn granite steps that led to the water's edge. Scrabbling clear of the water he reached the top, where he stumbled onto a loose gravel path that forked left and right.

Which way?

"Felta, oag felta," a voice snapped from below him.

Jack looked down but could see nothing.

"Felta, owan ruyhar!"

The impatient voice seemed to be coming from a knotted tree-stump.

"Ruyhar!"

Jack blinked, unable to believe what he was seeing. The stump looked like it had a face, a face of a one-eyed hag with a scarf wrapped tightly over her head. The eye was straining to the left, then back to him, and then left again.

Is she trying to give me directions? Does she mean left?

Jack couldn't understand a single word that came from her wooden lips but her tone was urgent and he couldn't ignore it. Left it was. His boots dislodged damp clumps of gravel as he ran. He ducked overhanging branches and leapt waterlogged gullies until he reached a wild grassy patch, no bigger than his bedroom. Halfway across it, the ground suddenly disappeared from beneath him. Jack's belly lurched and a terrible taste filled his mouth as he fell, landing heavily on his already battered knees.

It took a while for Jack to register what had happened. The walls of his trap were over eight feet high, glass-smooth, and solid as rock. He coughed and spluttered, as he looked around, trying to catch his breath. There was no escape. They, whatever they were, had caught him and he was at their mercy but by the sounds coming from above they didn't know what mercy was.

The screeching and screaming was becoming more and more frenzied. Jack crouched in a corner, trying to block it out by ramming his fingers in his ears, but eventually he could stand it no longer.

"Shut up!" he roared. "Just shut up… shut up… shut up… whatever the heck you are, just….."

A flash of light tore across the sky, sending Jack scuttling back to his corner. Gradually the agonising caterwauls began to fade into the distance. Had he done that? Had he sent them packing? Jack waited. What now?

There was a short silence before Jack noticed a thin rope of knotted ivy being dropped down into the pit. He sprang to his feet, his fists clenched, and waiting for his captors. But nobody – and nothing - came. He tugged the rope and it held, so he decided to climb. The muscles in his arms strained as he inched higher and higher towards what he hoped might be freedom. Finally, exhausted, he threw his elbow over the edge and hauled himself out. He lay on the ground, panting. The creatures had gone. But when he sat up he realised that he was hopelessly lost. He had no idea what direction he'd come from. He shuddered with cold and tiredness. His fingers were frozen, his toes numb and his stomach was begging for food.

Surely, his Ma would be out looking for him.

He went to cry for help, but stopped himself, worried that he would only bring back the screaming creatures. He peered into the darkness in all directions but saw nothing, except… there… yes, there in the distance, there was a fleeting glimmer of light. Aching all over, he began to walk towards it.

Chapter 7

Tree in the Tree

Jack had never seen anything like this before. A gigantic oak tree, bigger than anything he could ever have imagined, thrust into the night sky. Its towering trunk and widening branches twisted upwards as if trying to touch the stars. Its massive roots gripped the earth beneath his feet.

How high was it? Did it go on forever? He peered up through the foliage, but he couldn't make out where the tree ended and the sky began, and he feared his neck would snap if it bent any further back.

Suddenly a ray of moonlight lit the clearing, and Jack saw a smaller tree nestling inside the trunk of the mighty oak, as though it had been carved out of the great tree. Branches - tiny in comparison to those above - seemed to reach into the heart of the huge tree in which it was sheltering.

A tree growing inside a tree, thought Jack. *Impossible.*

Fanned by a breeze the branches creaked like the boards of a ship, and the sound of glass wind chimes tinkled from somewhere overhead. Jack squinted up into the smaller tree's canopy and caught a faint flicker of light, but before he could make out the source, an intense glare, brighter than any he had experienced before, even brighter than the lighthouse off the shores of Annalong, scorched the darkness, forcing his eyes closed.

Jack waited, terrified. Finally, he dared to open his eyes. It took a few moments, but once his eyes adjusted to the daylight, he looked slowly upwards through the branches of the little oak tree until he focused on an extraordinary sight.

A lopsided wooden-planked mansion, a hundred times the size of his cottage, teetered upon the tree's twisting boughs. Stilts jutted out here and there, shoring up the sagging edges of the building. It was as though an angry storm had swept the house up into the tree and abandoned it here.

Stained glass in the crooked bay windows threw multicoloured shadows onto the elevated walkways that surrounded the house. A tower wrapped in a ladder of cast-iron leaned against the house and at its peak, a beam blazed like a fiery white inferno.

"Scrrrraaaaawk… scrrrraaaaaawk."

They were back! The terrifying screeches swooped down towards him. Protecting his head with his arms, he dashed to the base of the tree, forcing his body into the bark's deep crevices, trying to find shelter. In his panic, his head hit the tree but it wasn't wood he had struck. Spinning around he saw a small pane of glass.

"Let me in… let me in!"

He pressed his nose hard against the window, pounding his fists against the smudged glass until he thought he could hear muffled footsteps from inside. He stumbled backwards, unsure whether to run away, or to wait and see whose footsteps they were. Before he could decide, the tree's bark split open and Jack found himself in some kind of a doorway. The screeching birds swooped once again. Should he make a run for it?

He hesitated for a split second before something reached out, grabbed him by his belt, and dragged him inside.

Chapter 8
The Clurichaun

Jack lashed out, panic-stricken. His arms and legs flailed but they didn't connect with anything. The door slammed behind him and he made a frenzied grab for the handle but before he could reach it the edges of the doorframe faded away. He clawed at the wood but it was futile, no trace of an escape remained.

"Meaha!" It sounded like someone coughing.

"Who's there?" shouted Jack.

"Meaha!"

The second cough was louder and more deliberate than the first and this time Jack could tell where it came from... He looked down. A creature stood holding a lit candle. It was no taller than Jack's chest, and that even included the oversized hat that sat upon its head. Ancient eyes peered up from under the rim but the face Jack was staring at belonged to a child. Shaggy raven hair fell in thin braids interwoven with a bead or two from the edges of its forehead. It had a pale complexion, all except for its cheeks, which were as rosy red as orchard apples. A tiny goatee beard grew beneath its lower lip.

A beard on a child, thought Jack, fascinated.

Around its thin neck, Jack noticed a golden torc engraved with a Celtic rope pattern. It was the same as the design carved on the cornerstone of his house. Over a white linen shirt, laced up the front, the creature wore a patchwork waistcoat of herringbone and check tweed. From the look of it, it lived in hand-me-downs that had seen better days. The glint of a golden chain caught Jack's eye. It dangled from a small pocket and fastened at the other end to a buttonhole with what looked like copper stitching. Jack smiled for an instant when he noticed that from its scuffed black boots sprang stripy socks of green and yellow. They stretched above its knees until they met the hem of a faded pair of red woollen britches, patched here and there with a purple material. Jack could not help noticing they were very poorly darned at the knees.

It was only when he looked back to the hat, that Jack noticed two pointed ears sticking out through the brim.

"Reay'ou afesa woan," the creature said.

It drew nearer and Jack stepped back. Couldn't it hear the horrific screaming and screeching still coming from outside? Jack had no idea what it was saying. Could he trust it? It held out a small stubby hand, as though to greet him, but Jack was having none of it and shoved his hands into his pockets.

There was a short pause. Then the creature spoke again. "Mocea hawit ema." Its tone was welcoming and it smiled a smile so warm and friendly that Jack decided that it surely meant him no harm. Cautiously he took his right hand out of his pocket.

"P…p…pleased to meet you," he said.

The creature smiled even more widely and gently and firmly shook Jack's hand. It was obviously pleased to have won his guest's trust.

Ignoring the continuous screeching from outside the tree, the creature beckoned Jack to follow him up the stairs. Jack knew he'd no option but to follow. Whatever it was outside sounded like it wanted to kill him and the only way out that he was aware of was sealed. Besides, he was sure that he could smell warm cinnamon toast. He followed the creature up a long spiral staircase. On every polished step, there were hundreds of tiny glass jars, each one shimmering with a magical glow. Jack lost count as he climbed. With every turn, he had to move quicker to keep up, each step approaching faster and faster until he was moving at a dizzying speed, gripping the banister as he went. He was desperate not to lose the creature in the hat.

Just when he thought he was about to faint, the stairwell came to an abrupt end and Jack stumbled out into a grand hallway. Although he had stopped, inside his head everything kept moving, whirling, and toppling in on him. Terrified, he threw his arms over his head and closed his eyes.

After a short while, the spinning eased. He lowered his arms and got to his feet, scanning the room. Oak shelves stacked full with leather bound books lined the walls, running long ways, length ways, and every-which-ways. At the end of the hall a double spiral staircase, grander than anything Jack had ever seen rose from the floor. Behind it stretched a long stained glass window showing a small tree inside a large tree. When he looked up beyond the top of the window, Jack could see hundreds of thin wooden rafters reaching into the pinnacle of the roof, like the underside of a ginormous mushroom.

Something tugged on Jack's sleeve, and Jack looked down to where the creature was gazing up at him, smiling. He led him down the hall until he stopped and turned to look at one of the bookcases. There he pointed up to a red leather bound book.

Jack frowned. "Do you want me to get it for you?"

The creature pointed again. Jack reached up and pulled the book towards him. There was a loud click and the bookcase swung out revealing a secret door. Jack stepped back quickly but the creature, smiling even more broadly, ushered him inside a small study where a great log fire crackled and sizzled, spitting scarlet flames up a vast chimney. Smiling, the creature bowed briefly, and then promptly disappeared.

Jack looked around him. Where was he? Patterned plates and misshapen candlesticks sat upon the mantelpiece, and carved into it was the image of a tree inside a tree, the same as the stained glass window in the hall. Nailed below the carving hung a row of silver spoons, each with a different handle. Jack counted eleven in all. Each had a large hole making them impossible to drink from.

On each wall, there was a painting of a small bear wearing a patchwork flat cap and waistcoat. A watch chain hung from its waistcoat pocket. Jack couldn't help grinning. What sort of people lived here?

A writing bureau sat at an angle in a corner. Jack walked over to take a closer look but he didn't touch. What looked like lots of rough sketches bulged from small pigeonholes and detailed maps poked out from half-opened drawers below.

Jack turned slowly round, taking in every detail. Just wait until he told his Ma about this! All of a sudden he had the uncomfortable feeling he was being watched. He swung round. On the wall behind him hung what looked like a family portrait – every eye was on him. Jack recognised one of them as the tiny creature that had just saved his life. He approached the painting with an outstretched hand and was an inch from the canvas when the door of the study burst open. Jack's hand flew to his side.

"Reaha. Kinrad astih."

The creature in the hat held out a small earthenware bowl brim full of liquid. Jack gulped down mouthful after mouthful, coughing and spluttering as he quenched his thirst.

"There now, that's better isn't it?"

"Yes… but…" Jack was stunned." You speak my language!'

The creature nodded. "Welcome to the Curraghard Tree, young one. May it be too small to hold all your friends, but may you live long enough to fill it."

In a grand gesture, it swept off its hat and bent on one knee.

"Th…Th…Thank you," replied Jack, a little embarrassed.

"I am Cosabian Broghan Hawksbeard but it has been too many whiles since anyone called me that and anyway it's too much of a mouthful. Just call me Cobs."

Jack smiled at the lilt of its voice. "Hello Cobs."

"You're safe here, in my home and a most welcome guest. This is where I live when I'm not out hunting."

Hunting what? Thought Jack.

"And you are?"

"I'm… I'm… just Jack… Jack Turner," he stuttered, "Wha…what was in that drink you gave me?"

"Now I wouldn't say I gave you it. More like you tore it from my hands. It's an herbal brew. The recipe was handed down to my mother by her mother and hers before that. It's given to all the newborns to help us know what we want even before we can speak. Since you're only a child I thought it might…"

"…I'm not a child! I'm eleven years old!" Jack retorted.

Cobs laughed. "Eleven! No blinkin' wonder it worked. I didn't start talking 'til I was fifty and that was after a good couple of doses of that potion."

"Fifty! What do you mean you were Fifty? What age are you now?"

"Let me see. My father, Poitin, carved the tree, so, so long ago. Before I was born even. I don't ever remember coming to it but funny enough I always remember being here… Anyway, that's not the point… Ah yes. My age, that's what you asked me…Yes that's right…Four hundred and thirty seven years old, give or take a month. I'm the youngest of nine, don't you know." Cobs turned to the painting of his family. "They're all my brothers and sisters. That's Fearnog, the eldest. Beith, my only sister. Trom, Cuileann, Malip, Coll, Iur and the last but one, and by far the smartest, Crann Cno. This is my mother, Blaithnaid and that is Poitin, my father. They're all gone now…" Cobs stopped and quickly changed the subject. "I…. I hope you like the fire. It's mighty powerful. The logs are from a branch of the inner tree that re-grows overnight."

"That's fantastic. I mean a tree that grows inside a tree. Who ever heard of such a thing?"

"It's the Hawksbeard crest you know. A tree inside a tree. You'll find the symbol all over the house."

"The house is amazing too. A house on top of a tree that grows inside a tree. It's all so hard to believe. And this study is full of so many things, most of which I've never seen before and if you don't mind me asking, why are there so many pictures of a bear on the walls?"

"Ah, you mean Cobs. They named me after him. A great honour, my father said. He knew the bear a long time ago, long before he even met my mother. He said the bear saved his life once and they became great friends after that. My father wrote many stories about him," Cobs explained.

"But there aren't any bears in Ireland."

"Not now maybe but there were a long time ago."

"Really…" said Jack astonished.

"But none quite like Cobs." Cobs looked fondly at one of the paintings before turning back to his guest. "So Jack, you didn't come here through the Gothic or Barbican Gates. If you had, the Wizard of Durham would have found a way to tell me. No, you've come into this forest another way haven't you?"

"To tell you the truth I've no idea how I got here," said Jack.

"Well that didn't stop you. If I'm correct, you've come here by a way long since forgotten by your kind."

"My kind!" said Jack. "What do you mean my kind?" The little creature's dismissive tone was insulting. He looked it up and down. "What are you anyway? A leprechaun?"

It was Cobs' turn to be insulted. "Leprechaun! Leprechaun! How dare you! I'm a Clurichaun. A cousin of a leprechaun maybe, but that's as far as it goes."

"I'm sorry. It's just… I really have no idea how I got here. I don't even know where here is. All I know is that the journey was terrifying."

"You're in The Kingdom of Mourne, Jack. You're in the True Kingdom - the only Kingdom."

"But how did I get here? All I did was touch a mouldy old dandelion – which dragged me through my own front door."

"And where is this door?"

"In Annalong, where I come from."

"Is there anything unusual about it?" Cobs was peering at Jack now.

"No, nothing. It's just my front door."

"There must be something about it, Jack, something you have forgotten. Think hard. Is there anything unusual about your home?"

"No, nothing, like I said, it's just my home... No wait a minute." He didn't want to think about her at this particular moment, but from the look on Cobs' face, it was vital that he tell him everything he knew. "There is one thing. Nanna Tess – she's my Da's Grandma - told me the stones in the archway of the front door came from quite a distance. They used a different stone for the archway from the rest of the house."

"And where did the rocks come from?"

"Nanna told me it had come all the way from Tollymore Forest."

"Tollymore Forest!" Cobs raised his eyebrows and rubbed his chin. "That explains it."

"Explains what?"

"How you got here."

"How?"

"This is Tollymore Forest."

"What!"

"Yes this is Tollymore Forest, but it's not exactly as you may know it."

Cobs went to a cupboard and lifted something out.

"What do you mean?" asked Jack.

"Never mind. Here –" Cobs unwrapped a slice of pie, "- eat this. You look famished."

Jack sat down on an overstuffed armchair and feasted on the most amazing pie he had ever tasted. The apples were stewed to perfection with just the right amount of sugar and cinnamon. The pastry, crusty-edged and slightly overdone, just the way he liked it.

Cobs, delighted at the way the boy was tucking into the pie, pointed to the cupboard. "It's a great larder. Nothing ever rots in it and it always seems to have just what you crave."

Jack nodded enthusiastically. It wasn't polite to thank somebody with your mouth full.

"About that trap earlier," Cobs continued. "It was actually meant for me... When I heard the commotion outside I knew the Drinns must have caught something. I'm glad you got the rope I threw down but I must apologise for not waiting for you to come out."

"That was you? Thank you!" replied Jack, wiping his mouth with the back of his hand. "I didn't know what was chasing me."

"Ah yes. Beware the Drinns my young friend. Yours is the flavour they crave the most."

"You mean they really would have eaten me?" said Jack, appalled.

"No, no, no, nothing like that. The Drinns are a kind of bird, but they've no wings or claws, or feathers for that matter. In fact, they aren't really birds at all, but they can fly - I think. They're something that pretends to be a bird; well at least they sound like a bird to me."

"They sounded nothing like birds," said Jack. "They sounded more like -like the worst thing you've ever heard."

Cobs nodded. "That's how they work. They feed off your fear. If you saw them in the daylight, you'd probably die laughing. They stand no higher than a chicken but lower than a dog, they smell of poultice bandage and I'm told they taste of frog."

"What!"

"Sorry, it's an old ditty about the Drinns. I think Trom or Malip made it up. They're a nocturnal breed. That flash of light is how I scared them away earlier. They would have just hung around their trap making you more and more terrified."

"Well, thank you for making that light to make sure they'd run off." Jack shook his head at the memory.

"No Jack…" Cobs faltered, his voice trailing off. His eyes looked sad all of a sudden. Then he brightened. "I… I mean yes. Yes, that's why I lit the lamp in the lighthouse!"

Something told Jack that Cobs wasn't telling the whole truth but he didn't press the matter any further.

Cobs hopped down from the chair, rifled through some of the sketches in the writing bureau and lifted out a piece of paper.

"Here, this is a Drinn," he said, handing Jack a sketch.

"This is what Drinn looks like? This is what I was so frightened of?" Jack laughed so hard his ribs ached and he had to force himself to stop.

"I know. Ridiculous creatures, aren't they? But Jack, I still don't know, how did you get here?" Cobs' voice became low and serious.

Jack looked down at his boots. "You won't laugh will you?"

"No, of course not. I promise."

"Well… I made this wish, you see."

"A wish?"

Jack told Cobs the story of the wish Nanna Tess had given him for his tenth birthday. "I couldn't wait for my second wish – for my eleventh birthday," he explained. "I'd had all kinds of ideas but there was a storm, you see, the worst one my Ma says she's ever seen. It was the night before my eleventh birthday and my Da was out fishing at sea. The next day they found his boat but he was not on board. They say he's lost at sea. Old man Russell told my Ma that there was no way a man could survive such a storm."

Cobs was staring at the fire embers almost as if he'd lost something there, just like Nanna Tess would often do. He was silent.

"Cobs?" Jack wondered if he'd fallen asleep.

"Sorry." The little man snapped out of his thoughts and turned to Jack. He clapped his hands together. "I think it's time for bed."

"But I can't stay. My mother will be looking everywhere for me. She'll be worried sick," said Jack.

"I promise you, Jack that she will hardly notice you're gone. Time does funny things this side of your archway."

For some reason Jack believed him, even if he didn't quite understand him. Perhaps it was because he felt so tired and he wanted to believe Cobs, or maybe it was because he didn't think the little man was capable of lying. Anyways, he decided to stay and that night Jack lay under a silken eiderdown, in a hammock that hung from two branches growing right out of knots in the floorboards. His head rested on a pillow filled with fine lavender sand and next to him, he laid his toy, the broken boat his father had made him. Soon he drifted into the deepest sleep he had ever known.

The morning sunshine woke him but he kept his eyes closed, enjoying the feeling of the warm rays. He could hear birdcalls outside and he tried to figure out what they belonged to. It wasn't long before the smell of porridge began to filter in from under the door. He made to get out of bed, but he forgot where he was. The hammock swung wildly back and forth, tossing him out onto the floor. Luckily for Jack a thick mattress lay directly beneath him and softened his fall.

That wasn't there last night, he thought but he was grateful all the same.

He walked to an open window and looked out. A low cloud hung over the dazzling sun, underneath which a mountain, cloaked in purple heather, rose majestically from the golden sand of the curved coastline. Way out at sea Jack could make out a flotilla of boats in full sail, riding hard on the morning breeze.

"Come and get it!" Cobs called from downstairs. "It's getting cold on the table and if there is one thing Drinns like better than fear it's…"

Jack got dressed, put his boat back in his pocket and ran down for breakfast. Cobs chuckled as Jack sat himself down.

"That's not funny, you know." Jack was still spooked at the thought of the screaming creatures from the night before.

"You're right, and I'm sorry for it." But Cobs couldn't help smiling.

Jack shook his head but after two enormous spoonfuls of delicious porridge, his mind turned to other things. "By the way, how did a mattress get under my bed? You could have let me sleep on it in the first place."

"Only babies sleep on the floor and the last time I met one of your kind they injured their leg falling out of that very hammock. You were out like a light by the time I remembered, so I crept into your room while you slept and put it there for this morning."

"You've met my kind before?"

"Yes. You're not the first." Cobs opened a drawer and handed Jack a wooden spoon carved with a picture of a young girl sitting at a table just like the one at which Jack was sitting, in front of a large steaming bowl. "Yes, many whiles ago. She liked hot cinnamon porridge and stewed apple too. Now eat."

Jack lifted his spoon and shovelled spoonful after spoonful into his mouth, like a train driver stoking an engine. "How do I get home, Cobs?" he asked, once he'd finished. "I need to get back to my Ma."

"You sure you won't stay a while? Like I've told you, she won't know you're gone for quite some time yet and besides I don't often get company. If you stay I'll show you some really amazing things, like my father's cloak and my compass."

"No, thanks all the same but I think I'd better be getting home." Just saying the words aloud gave him heart.

But Cobs sighed. "Grand so, if'n that's what you want. We'll even take the short cut, get you there quicker."

After breakfast, Jack followed Cobs to the top of the spiral staircase and pointed towards a curved tube that ran along side its top post. Without further ado, he sat on the edge and within a blink, disappeared.

"Come on," he shouted, his voice echoing in the distance.

There was nothing else for it. Jack sat on the edge and pushed off, just as Cobs had done. Surely this would be better than the hectic ascent of the stairs the previous evening. He heltered and skeltered downward barely making out his feet below him, the ever-increasing speed kept his head pressed firmly against the wooden floor, spinning even faster this time. Jack hit the bottom in what seemed like an instant, his head, and stomach arriving some moments later.

"Isn't it a great slide?" said Cobs, who was waiting for him. "My father carved it for us when we complained that it took us forever to answer the door."

The door that had disappeared behind Jack the day before was there, as if it always had been, and Jack and Cobs stepped through it and out of the Curraghard tree. Great swards of bluebells stood upright around them, almost as if to attention. Cobs led the way. Wrens and robins flitted from branch to branch on nearby trees and Jack saw fallow deer peering out from the thick bracken, watching them walking down the hillside to the waters edge.

"This is the river Shimna, Jack. We're lucky this morning. She whispers. Sometimes she babbles, but often she rages."

Jack nodded, remembering. "Look Cobs, do you see those stones." He pointed to where the pillars had emerged.

"But that's not … I've never seen them before…" the wee man stammered.

Jack could tell that Cobs was astonished at the sight. "They rose out of the water last night when I was being chased by the Drinns."

"Impossible!"

"No it's not. It really happened. I swear. I thought I was going to dro…" Jack stopped mid sentence. "The rocks just... appeared. They saved my life."

"But that means…..... No matter, come on." Cobs skipped from stone to stone until he reached the other side. "Your turn now."

Jack firmly planted both his feet on each rock before he took the next step.

"We're nearly there, Jack."

"What were you going to say just then? You said 'that means.'… then you stopped?"

"The river knows something about you, Jack. I don't know what, but for her to have helped you, she must have thought you worthy." Cobs didn't speak again until they reached the ruins of the ancient cottage where Jack had arrived. He stopped and turned to Jack. "I can show you how to get home now. All you have to do is hold the rock and think of the doorway of your cottage. These rocks are one and the same, and you'll be there in an instant."

Jack didn't question how Cobs knew what to do, he was too grateful for a way home.

"Thank you Cobs," said Jack holding on to a cold damp rock. He couldn't wait to get home now.

"It was very good to meet you," said Cobs. He held up his hand for a moment. "Just one thing, Jack, before you go."

"What's that?"

"Don't you want to know why your wish – the second wish - didn't come true?"

Jack released the rock, a feeling of dread taking hold of his middle. "What do ya mean?"

"Something strange has just happened Jack." Cobs leant against one of the ruined walls. He nodded in the direction of the route they'd just taken. He was no longer smiling. "The river has proved that. There's more to you than has ever met an eye."

Jack shrugged. What did Cobs mean?

"I know why your wish didn't come true. But if I tell you, you'll not want to leave and the journey you'd have before you, could be your last."

Jack turned to face his new friend. "You're telling me my wish could still come true?" he said, his face beaming. "Da might come back?"

"Yes," said Cobs hesitantly. "But -"

Jack felt a sudden rush of excitement. "No buts, just tell me what I have to do!"

"Are ya sure? Do you want it enough to risk - ?"

"Of course! It's what I want more than anything in the world!"

"Are ya sure you're sure?"

Cobs looked hard at Jack, and then he walked slowly away.

"Cobs! I've never been more positive about anything in my life. If you can help..." Jack's heart was in his mouth.

Cobs stopped walking and turned. "If this is really what you want, just follow me."

Chapter 9

The Riddle

Jack followed Cobs back to the Curraghard tree, up the crazy spiral staircase and into the study they'd been in the night before. He watched intently as Cobs pressed on a wooden side panel of the writing bureau in the corner of the room. It popped open. Jack's eyes widened. Cobs lifted out an empty black iron pot about the size of a fruit bowl and handed it to him.

"What is it?" said Jack, baffled.

"What is it! What is it! That, ya young whippersnapper is only the most important thing to my kind." Cobs was clearly upset by Jack's ignorance.

"Well, why don't you tell me then? I don't know what this thing is. I've never seen it before in my life."

"I've a good mind not to."

"Well then don't." Jack was near to tears. Had he made a terrible mistake? Was Cobs the friend he believed he was?

"Well just to spite ya I'm gonta tell ya even more than ya need to know. That pot you're holding would once have been overflowing with gold, but not any longer. We left all that gold stuff to the Leprechauns a long time ago. There is something we collect now that's more precious than gold."

"More precious than gold! Nothing's more precious than gold!"

"Jack. Steady on now. This isn't your world we're in now. It's mine. And I'm about to tell you about something more precious than any treasure you could ever imagine. Dandelion clocks."

"Dandelion clocks?"

"Yes. Every time a wish is made on a dandelion, just like the way your Nanna Tess taught you, each and every one of the clocks that are blown off must be collected before that wish can come true. That is why Tess told you the Silver Orb had to be freed of clock."

Jack recalled the riddle his great grandmother had read to him. "But how could you know that?"

"It's an ancient poem and the only way you could have made it into this forest was by doing what it said."

"But if I did it right then what happened to my wish? It didn't come true. My father never came home."

"Something bad happened to your wish Jack. Remember I told you I go hunting?"

Jack nodded.

"Well, it's dandelion clocks that I hunt. You see, it's been my family's duty for thirteen generations to collect those dandelion clocks, so that the wishes can come true." Cobs paced up and down in front of the fireplace. "But these days, I often find that a single clock is missing, one here, and another there. It's not that often now I catch all the clocks. All those jars you saw on the stairs Jack, every one of them is missing a clock so the wish can't come true. They sit there glowing, waiting. Someone's stealing them jack, but I have no idea who or why."

"We have to find out and that's all there is to it. You've no idea how important this wish is to me!" declared Jack.

"But there's a hundred years of wishes on those stairs waiting to come true, what makes you think that you can find the missing dandelion clock to make your wish come true?"

"I didn't say I could but I'll die trying."

Cobs shook his head wearily. He was thinking hard. Then he looked up at Jack. "Do you know something? Having witnessed what I just did back at the river, you might be the first glimmer of hope that I've had in a long, long time."

"What do ya mean?"

"I've heard about those river stones before, but I've never seen them. Nor have I known anybody who has. But the River Shimna has revealed her greatest secret to you; she saved your life last night and that means only one thing. She cares for you. That's good enough for me."

"So where do we go next?" asked Jack, impatient to get going. Much as he liked Cobs' beautiful house, he wanted to get on with the task he had set himself. Cobs looked at the floor for a few moments. "Ah," he said carefully. "There's one person in the forest who'll know how to help you."

"Then let's go and talk to him."

Cobs nodded heavily. "It's a her. She is called Erica Tetralix but we haven't spoken to each other in a lifetime. In fact after what happened I don't think we'll ever speak again."

Jack clutched at his head. Everything Cobs said created new problems! "What do you mean? She might speak to me. I'll do anything to make my wish come true, Cobs. Anything!"

"Well, this time of year our best chance of finding her is at the Ivy Bridge but you must meet her alone Jack. If she has an inkling I'm with you I know she won't help."

In the end, Jack persuaded Cobs to come along, even if he refused to attend the meeting at the Ivy Bridge.

Cobs packed everything they needed for their journey. They were just about to set off when he looked at Jack. "You can't go out like that. You wouldn't last a tick in the hills. You have to be ready for what the seasons may throw at you, Jack." The little man thought for a moment. "You're lucky, my father was considered tall for my kind, and you, by the looks of it, are very small for yours. I think his clothes may be a good fit for you. Come."

Jack wanted to say something smart but he kept quiet, for he had to admit that he was on the small side. Cobs lead the way down several passages until they reached a bedroom in the middle of which sat a huge five-poster bed, heavily carved with scenes of Tollymore Forest. Cobs set to work, pulling clothes out of the cupboards.

Jack was distracted by a carving on the bed. "Cobs, look. On this picture, there's the stones that helped me cross the Shimna River."

Cobs came and stared at the carving. "That's impossible." He rubbed it with his thumb. "Those stones weren't there last time I was in here polishing. It was just a carving of the river, plain and simple. It's another sign, Jack. This must have something to do with you." He pulled more clothes out of the cupboard and threw them onto the bed. He was in a hurry. "Here, try these on. They belonged to my father."

Jack picked up a shirt and rubbed it against his cheek. "I can't wear this. It's itchier than my Da's jumper."

Cobs laughed. "You'll be glad of it at night. I could spit through that shirt of yours and that's saying something considering my kind can't spit."

"What!"

"Long story and no time to tell it, now come on."

Jack was pleased so see Cobs in brighter spirits. Once he'd changed, Cobs stood him in front of a full-length mirror framed with intricate Celtic knot work. Instead of his reflection, Jack could see straight through it to the other side of the room.

"What are you up to? This isn't a mirror."

Without answering, Cobs reached up and pressed a small carving of a squirrel on the left hand side of the frame. Liquid silver began to pour down to create a thin sheet, like a shimmering waterfall. Jack gazed at the reflection. His cotton shirt had been replaced by fine linen, tied in thin criss-cross cords to his neck. Over it, he was wearing a faded but elaborately decorated waistcoat, its pockets baggy as though regularly stuffed with useful objects.

Jack's hand rested on a braided belt around his waist, where an empty leather scabbard was fixed. He felt for a knife but there was none. A cape the colour of grey slate fell from his shoulders but its dull exterior was more than made up for by a lining of the most vibrant green silk he'd ever seen. A spike of hawthorn pierced the cloth near his right shoulder holding in place a silver brooch that bore the crest of the Hawksbeard family, the tree within the tree.

"It's woven from the wool of the Clan Caora Jack. That cape will keep you dry no matter the weather and if you turn it inside out no creature will be able to tell you apart from countryside."

Jack looked at the lining more closely. "It must have more than forty shades of green."

"It does Jack. Twas my father's most prized possession. Got him out of many a scrape."

Jack looked down to his ankles and smiled. Striped stockings like those that Cobs wore, ran up his legs and disappeared under the hem of the brown britches that hung just below his scabby knees. His own boots, scuffed and worn, didn't look much out of place.

Cobs looked pleased with what he saw. "We're ready to go Jack."

Cobs had packed for every season but in backpacks no bigger than school bags.

"Whatever you're thinking of taking on a trip Jack, half it, then half it again and after that if you've any sense half it once more. It's best to travel light and use whatever comes to hand, it's worked for me up till now."

Jack smiled. He'd never travelled further than his own back yard, as his mother used to say and now he was going on an adventure.

They stood in the doorway to the tree.

"Can you taste that, Jack?"

"What?"

"The great outdoors," Cobs laughed. "Come on."

Jack hesitated for a moment. He was about to set off on the most important journey of his life and the thought scared him. What if he failed? It didn't bare thinking about. He took a sharp intake of breath and tried to put any negative thoughts from his mind.

"I'm coming," Jack shouted, trying to sound brave.

They followed the long course of the river Shimna, flanked by a solid mass of bright sugar-scented azalea, past deep rock pools, and cascading waterfalls and after a few minutes they came to the bridge.

"There it is," whispered Cobs." The Ivy Bridge. You go on, I'll wait here."

"Come with me." Jack couldn't help asking.

"I can't. I told you already, if Erica Tetralix knows I'm with you, she'll tell you nothin'."

"But why Cobs, what happened?"

Cobs shifted about and Jack could see he was making him nervous." Now's not the time Jack, just go on if you want the answer to your question."

"I need to know. I mean, what happened to my wish?"

"Then go on and ask her. I'll wait here for you."

The creeping ivy had long since eaten away the stones of the bridge, and now its arched vines spanned the river. Jack had an immediate distrust of the structure but he placed the tip of his boot onto it and to his surprise, it didn't budge. It stood as solid as any rock, so he crossed to its centre and looked over the edge, at the river as it plunged and splashed below. The spray seemed to dance in front of his eyes and he began to feel a little giddy.

All of a sudden, Jack felt something sharp hit his arm. "What the..." He swung round and saw Cobs preparing to lob another stone at him.

"Jack! Jack!" he was calling. "She's not here. Come back!"

"Ouch. What'd ya do that for?" Jack rubbed his arm as he walked back towards Cobs.

"You were standing there as if you had all the time in the world, Jack," said Cobs.

"I was not! I was just thinking. There was no need to throw those stones." Jack frowned at Cobs.

"You've been waiting there for over an hour Jack, I couldn't leave you there any longer. The waters must have hypnotised you."

"What! But I've only been gone a minute."

"No Jack, I could have grown a full beard in the time you've..." Cobs stopped. He could see that Jack was at the end of his tether. He patted the boy on the shoulder, guiding him away. "It was for the best, you'll see," he soothed.

"Alright, alright, but where is she, the one person you said could help me? What am I supposed to do now? You bring me all the way here and she doesn't show up."

"I'm sorry, Jack, that she's not here. There's only one other place she'll be this time of year."

"I hope you're right this time," said Jack, still annoyed. But he knew he had no choice but to follow Cobs. Neither of them spoke as they walked through a small beech wood and crossed onto a track that veined its way upwards through the gorse bushes on the hillside.

A few moments later, Cobs stopped and pointed ahead. "This is the Trassey path, Jack. And those over there are the cliffs of Spellak. This is the very route that the Wee Binnians took thousands of years ago, smuggling their brandy right under the noses of the dreaded Shimnavore. You'll have heard about all that, surely?"

Nanna Tess had told plenty of stories by the fire of an evening, and so had Matthew – but Jack had never heard of these characters. He shook his head. "Wee… what did you call them? And the Shimnavore, what the heck are they?"

Cobs eyes widened. "You've never heard of the Shimnavore? They were only the most deadly beasts to stand on Irish soil." Now he shook his head, but in disbelief. He began to walk on. "Thankfully, they're long since extinct."

Jack breathed a sigh of relief and followed. "I'm glad then that I'll never meet them. And by the way why are we going this way?"

"You'll find out soon enough, I promise, just have a little faith in me."

Leaving the forest behind them, they trampled over bog cotton and bedstraw, rising higher and higher into the mountainside. Cobs might be hundreds of years old, but he was fitter than Jack, his little legs striding ahead. Jack just began to wonder if he could ask for a short break when suddenly Cobs stopped. "Look, Jack."

Up ahead, in the centre of the track, was an iron gate. There was no fence to either side. It wasn't even attached to a post. Instead, the gate seemed to float in mid air, about a foot off the ground.

"That's funny," said Jack, about to step around it, "but with everything else I've seen here I'm starting to get used to seeing strange things."

"Stop!" said Cobs with an urgency that made Jack freeze on the spot, his left foot still in mid air. "You can't go round this gate. That would be a disaster! Bad luck would follow us the rest of our journey."

Jack stepped back, surprised by how agitated Cobs was. It was only a gate, after all!

But Cobs was adamant. "This is the gateway to the Mournes, Jack. It's not called the Kissing Gate for nothing you know. Now kiss the gate and then you can go through."

Jack reversed away from the gate, waving his hand. "No way!" He laughed. Cobs had gone too far now, surely.

"Just do it!" Cobs was deadly serious. His eyes showed real fear in a way that Jack hadn't seen since they'd met.

So Jack slowly made his way back up the hill, puckered his lips and laid them upon the bare rusted metal. Immediately, the gate opened silently on its hinges of air and the two of them passed through. For a while, Cobs seemed to relax, and the going was easier.

But it wasn't long before Jack could see that Cobs was becoming agitated again. The gravel path had turned into soft ground clothed in pale pink heather, worn here and there in places to expose barren grey rock.

"We're here Jack. Do you see those clumps of heather beneath your feet? Well they mean it's time I wasn't here. As I've already told you, if Erica Tetralix has got any idea I'm here she'll not speak to you."

Jack shrugged. "What did you two quarrel about any way? I mean, shouldn't you at least tell me?"

"What difference would it make Jack?"

"I'm here for my Da you know. I have to make my wish come true..."

Cobs narrowed his eyes and pointed into the distance.

"I know how important this is to you Jack, don't for a second think I don't." Cobs voice had a hint of irritation that didn't go unnoticed on Jack. "Way over yonder are the Dromara hills, Jack, but do you see that exposed tor? Go there, stand below it, and wait."

"Tor?" Jack still had no idea what Cobs was talking about.

"Yes, over there," said Cobs pointing to a standing rock formation in the distance. "That's the tor. And that's where she'll be." He sat himself down in the heather. It was obvious that he would say no more.

Jack made his way across the heath until he was in the Tor's shadow. Cobs had been wrong before, and Jack wasn't sure he was right this time. The longer he stood the more he worried about the woman he'd been told to wait for. How bad could she be? Bad enough if Cobs wouldn't risk meeting her. But he'd been so sure that she could help

Jack. He tried to distract himself by watching a family of red ants running about carrying huge leaves on their backs. Nothing got in their way. Nothing stopped them.

Suddenly Jack felt a movement beneath his feet, as if the ground was slowly shifting. At first, he paid it no attention, thinking it was only the marsh settling. The ants continued about their business, but there it was again. The ground moved but this time with more energy, and there was a sound now, as if it was groaning. He watched, bewildered, as the heather began to creep away from his boots. It started to swell upwards into a mound, and then grew higher still like a rising tide. Jack watched, his heart thumping, as tight clusters of the heather's flowers lifted above him. It all happened so fast that there was no chance of escape. He was pinned inside the heather as the loose peat turned and twisted around and above him.

Eventually the earth began to settle, releasing Jack and from it emerged something which gradually took shape until finally, standing in front of him was a tall lady, long robes of pink heather draped over her slender shoulders. Jack gazed up at her. She was more beautiful than anything he could ever have imagined. Her face was pale like the colour of milk but her hair was darker than any night he'd ever seen. It looked like she had a crown of diamonds on her head but these were not jewels, they were snail-trails glistening in the sun light. But it was the lady's eyes that particularly drew Jack's attention. They were completely grey, like stone. They told him nothing. Jack's heartbeat slowed when he looked into them.

"Hear me, young one, but not with your ears. You must open your mind."

Her crimson lips did not move and there was no noise, yet Jack could hear her clearly in his thoughts.

"I am Erica Tetralix, the second sister of the heather. You seek answers to riddles that must never be told and want truths that can't ever be spoken. Your path is best to return to the ancient ruins and go back home."

Jack bowed his head. This wasn't what he needed to hear. He raised his eyes again. "I can't return home. I need to know why my wish didn't come true. My Da..." He couldn't speak for the tears in his throat.

The lady said nothing. Terrified that she would disappear as suddenly as she had appeared, Jack knelt and touched her robe. "Won't you tell me?"

A single white flower of heather bloomed exactly where Jack's hand lingered. Astonished, he looked up at her. She was staring at the flower.

Finally she spoke. "This is not possible young one. The answer lies before you and you can't even see it." Her eyes still did not leave the flower on the hem of her robe. It was as if she was lost in her own thoughts.

Suddenly, from behind him Jack heard an urgent whisper. "Cinerea..." He twisted round but there was no one there. He looked up at the stoney eyes but the heather lady showed no sign of having heard anything.

She continued. "There is something inside you that has not revealed itself yet. You are blessed with the sight of the mountains. I cover their skin to give them warmth and they in turn feed me, but you have their sight! I will not give up their secrets but I will tell you this... You seek the way of the Mourne, but you must keep to the foothills, the walls are watching."

In a swift movement, she reached down and snapped her fingers up close to Jack's eyes, making him blink. When he opened them, the lady was holding out a tiny piece of parchment. He studied it briefly but the symbols meant nothing to him. He looked back to the lady to thank her and to ask her what it meant but she had vanished. In his mind he could hear her speak and although she was no longer there he could hear her words in his mind.

"The little one will show you. Tell him he cannot hide from me."

None the wiser, Jack made his way back to Cobs' hiding place and handed him the parchment.

"I can't understand it."

Cobs studied it for a moment. "It's written in Ogham, Jack; an ancient script." Then he read aloud.

> "Clock so vast,
>
> Lock so small,
>
> Open Drohan's,
>
> Creviced scrawl.
>
> Mountain piece and
>
> Orb so round,
>
> Rock that rests on higher ground."

Without any further comment, Cobs folded the parchment and put it in his waistcoat pocket. He got up and dusted himself down as if there was nothing further to say.   "Now – shall we get on our way?"

"Not until you explain... Do you know what it means, Cobs?"

The little man shrugged. "No. No more than you do. What else did she say to you, Jack? Did anything... untoward happen?"

Jack didn't know where to start. The moving earth? The heather enclosure? The way the lady had emerged? Her eyes?

"There was a white flower on the hem of her gown, where I touched it. I don't think she was expecting that... and then she told me I had a secret inside me, whatever that means. Oh, and that I must keep to the foothills in the morning. Sure, it's late afternoon now, isn't it Cobs? Oh – and she also said the walls were watching." Jack threw up his hands in dismay. "None of it makes any sense. How is all that nonsense going to help me?"

Cobs hopped about, nodding his head from side to side as he considered all that Jack had told him. He seemed quite pleased. "She's told you more that I'd ever hoped. She didn't mean morning, she meant Mourne."

"That's what I said. 'Morn'. Well morning, to be exact."

"No Jack, she meant Mourne, not as in morning but as in the Mourne Mountains. Erica Tetralix meant the Mourne Way. The Mourne Way is a route along the foothills. In fact, we're already on it, and she means for us to continue on its path." He smiled broadly. "Now isn't that good news, Jack" And Cobs set off, setting a course very wide of the Tor.

Jack followed. It was best that he didn't mention that Erica Tetralix knew Cobs had been hiding for he still didn't know what had happened between the two of them and he didn't want to scare Cobs off. Without Cobs' help, Jack's quest would end.

Chapter 10
Journey to the Castle

Jack and Cobs walked on for a few hours along a worn trail lined with blue bilberries. Cobs stopped suddenly. "Listen!" he said softly.

"What is it?"

"Can't you hear that? The sound of young ones' laughter?" He turned and pointed. "Look, just yonder, under the shadow of Meelmore Mountain, on that mound of woolly moss, there's two Leaf-footed bugs playing with a family of Tiger beetles. It's not every day you get to see that kind of play, you know. It wasn't that long ago they'd have been fighting over that bit of moss."

Jack had no interest in what his friend was talking aboutand his face gave him away.

Cobs smiled. "Is everything all right, Jack?"

Jack took a deep breath. "No it's not all right, I'm tired, I need to sit down, I don't even know where I'm going and I'm... not really very interested in bugs and beetles."

Cobs wagged a finger at him. "Ah! The first tinge of a whinge means the younger has a hunger and the only way to stop it is to feed it."

"What?" Jack slumped down onto the ground, but he couldn't help smiling.

"It's fish for tea, my friend. I know a place where the salmon leap from the waters and land, cooked and ready, onto your plate."

"Really?" The very idea made Jack's stomach rumble.

"No, of course not," Cobs laughed. He picked a handful of bilberries. "Here, these'll keep you going. Now stop your whining and come on." He hauled Jack to his feet, and the two of them set off once again. Up ahead they could hear the gurgling sound of water.

"This'll guide us to where were goin'," said Cobs as he stepped over a clear mountain stream. They followed it in the direction the water was flowing and in a short while, they came to a lake. The view was amongst the most beautiful Jack had ever seen. The early evening sunlight was glistening through the rustling reeds and bouncing off the still water. Cobs lifted a flat pebble from the lakeside path and skimmed it over the surface. It skipped eleven times before it sank. Jack gave him a round of applause, and Cobs made a bow.

"This is Fofanny Dam, Jack." He pointed to the other side. "If you look closely into the hillside over there, you can see where the Lamella live."

Jack looked at him blankly. "Lamella...?"

"Do they teach you youngsters nothing these days? The Lamella is a curious breed whose only purpose in life is to ensure these waters remain pure."

Jack could tell that Cobs was delighted to be the one to tell him. He followed him towards the edge of the dam where Cobs opened his backpack and removed a thin white stick no longer than his forearm. He examined it closely, and then shook it back and forth. With every shake it grew longer, until it eventually it was three times Jack's height.

"What's that?" Jack made sure he stood well clear as Cobs brandished the stick.

"This? My father made it for me, from the Frosted Ash tree near my home. Here, try it."

Jack took hold of the stick. It dipped first to one side, then the other, but never once did it fall from his hand.

"Not bad!" said Cobs.

"It's amazing." Jack studied the carved handle, shaped to fit into a palm, and came across a tiny hole. "What's this?"

Cobs knew exactly what he was talking about. "Take a look through it."

Jack lifted the handle to his eye and peered through the tiny aperture. "Well, what's so great about that?" he said, disappointed.

"You'll see. Now point it towards the water."

Jack looked through the tiny hole towards the lake this time. He squealed with delight. "Wow, that's amazing Cobs. Everything's so clear. It's like the water's not there and the fish are swimming in mid-air." He turned slightly. "There's a shoal of fish over there, must be fifty of them, all darting about."

"Now you know what my father gave me. It's a fishing rod like no other, Jack. There's no place to hide from this one."

Cobs took the rod back and checked behind him to make sure nothing could get caught in the line. He faced the area where Jack had seen the fish; his body turned about a quarter turn and he aimed the tip of the rod towards his target, just level with his eyes. He bent his arm and swiftly and smoothly, when the rod was almost vertical, he flicked his forearm forward with a slight movement of his wrist. The line shot out and within a second of the fly hitting the water, he had a bite. He tugged on the rod and out leaped a huge salmon.

Jack jumped up and down clapping his hands. "It's amazing."

"My father also showed me how to tie a fly that no fish could resist. We're eating well this evening. Off you go and gather some kindling for a fire. We've dinner to cook."

When Jack came back with an armful of wood Cobs removed two small flint stones from his backpack and cracked them together over the kindling. Soon the smell of delicious fish filled the air and it wasn't long before the two of them were lying on the ground patting their full stomachs. There was so much they couldn't even finish it.

"That was the best supper I've ever had," said Jack. He sat up. "Can I see if I can catch one?"

"Sure," said Cobs. He didn't move. "Just do what I did."

Jack carried the rod to the end of a small wooden pier, raised the handle of the rod to his eye, and looked towards the water. This time instead of a shoal of fish, he could see something big, caught amongst the reeds. As he watched, he could see it was trying to break free. Jack strained to get a clearer image, leaning further towards the edge, holding the rod closer to his face. What was it? He narrowed his eyes and his heart began to race. It looked like the outline of a man…

…it was his father!

Without thinking Jack took another step closer, only now there was no pier left and he plunged headlong into the freezing water. He tried to right himself and keep his head above the surface as he'd been taught, but instead he just floundered, panicking more and more. Deeper and deeper he sank, lungs begging for air, heart begging to see his father. Desperate, he breathed in, and lake water exploded into his lungs. The sound of rushing water filled his ears and as he fought to stay conscious, he swore he could hear someone calling out to him. The voice twisted and spun in his head as if trying to confess a deeply guarded secret. Jack strained to hear, to understand. But it was no use. With a flicker of daylight flashing before his eyes, Jack could fight no longer. The water was winning. He was about to give up the almighty struggle when a vague shapeless object reached down and hauled him from the icy clasp of the lake.

Jack wondered if his lungs were bursting as he felt himself being pushed onto his side. "It's alright. You're safe," he heard Cobs say. "You fell into the water but you're on firm ground now. Calm yourself. Breathe. Everything's going to be fine."

Jack felt the weight of Cobs' hands pressing repeatedly on his chest. On the fifth go, he threw up great mouthfuls of water. Cobs patted him on the back, making comforting noises as Jack lay exhausted on the ground. Slowly his breathing returned to normal.

"Come on Jack, the fire will dry you." Cobs helped the boy sit up and settled him, shivering, in front of the campfire. Steam rose from Jack's clothes although the outside of his cloak was bone dry. It had been no good to him in the deep waters.

Jack pulled the cloak closer around him. "Cobs, you won't laugh if I tell you something will you?"

The look on Cobs' face radiated relief at hearing the boy's voice. "No of course not, why?"

"When my foot got caught in some reeds in the lake I thought I'd never come up for another breath, not ever. But just before you pulled me out I heard someone cry out to me. I think I recognised the voice ..."

"Who do you think it was?"

"If I tell you, promise you won't think I'm mad."

"Of course I won't."

"When I was five years old, I was down at the pier watching my father go out to sea as I did every morning. It was winter. My mother was there and so was my brother Edmund. He was six at the time. When the boat disappeared from view, we all started to walk home but we were half way up the lane when Edmund realised he'd dropped his scarf. Ma had knitted one for each of us. He ran back to get it and we waited for him, but after a minute or two, he hadn't come back so we went back to the pier. He wasn't there. Ma began to panic and it was then that I noticed something floating under the water. I don't remember much else except I dived in to save him. I only know what happened next, from what I've been told. It was the last time I saw my brother. I was too upset to go to his wake or his funeral."

Cobs walked over to Jack and placed his arm around him. "No one your age should lose a loved one," he said quietly, "but life can be cruel. I know that."

"But Cobs, his voice, he spoke to me in the lake…"
"What did he say, Jack?"
"I think it was… something like 'clock more.' Yes that's right, 'clock more.'"
For a few moments Cobs sat there, thinking, then he jumped up in stunned surprise.   "That's it!"

"What's it?" asked Jack.
"The answer to the riddle. You've just said it."
"I don't understand."
"It's Cloc Mor."
"Yes, that's what I said."
"Not 'clock more' Jack. Not like a ticking clock. It means Cloc Mor. It's Irish. Don't you see? Cloc Mor means big stone. That must be what Erica Tetralix meant by the clock so vast. There is a giant granite rock that rests high above Ruari's castle at the end of the Mourne Way." Cobs did a little dance to himself, delighted at his discovery. "We must get going before the sun sets. I know you're weak Jack, but we've a bit of a distance to go yet before we can sleep."

The exhaustion must have shown on Jack's face.
"Don't worry though," Cobs reassured him. "I know somewhere along the way that'll help you."

After they'd finished the rest of the fish Cobs gathered up all their belongings and together they set off. Cobs made sure they kept to the lowlands, passing through a deep valley. Jack kept close behind him. He was still shocked by his experience in the lake. The image of his father haunted him but he kept it to himself. He didn't know how Cobs would react if he told him.

The valley stretched on for several miles and they trekked along the stony track, through grass and bracken, over winding streams and damp peat hags. Jack was flagging, but when they reached a bend in the track the view changed to reveal dazzling sunlight reflecting off a lake. Immediately Jack felt a little better. "Where are we now, Cobs?" he asked.

"That lake, Jack, covers the area once known as the Col of Deers Meadow. It was home to the Nairulis and Hornfels before the great flood wiped them out. You're looking at Spelga Dam. Let's stand here a while. Bathe in her glory, Jack, for she has the power to heal."

Jack closed his eyes. His weary body began to tingle as if being showered by a thousand tiny sparks. Almost immediately, his aches and pains faded, and it wasn't long before he felt strong enough to carry a mountain, let alone climb one.

He stretched out his arms. "I know I've only been standing here for a minute but I feel like I've just woken up after a great night's sleep," he told a delighted Cobs before marching on with a newfound spring in his step.

"That's great, Jack, because the light will be leaving us soon and I want to show you something before night falls." He stopped, and pointed. "You see that outcrop up there. That's where we'll be spending the night. Pierce's Castle."

The distance would have seemed far too far only ten minutes earlier, but Jack had enough energy now. They travelled along a clear track across grass and bracken towards the outcrop.

"I'm starting to get cold and to tell the truth, a bit tired," said Jack. "I'll be glad of a bed."

Cobs burst out laughing. "A bed, have you no sense of occasion?"

"What's the occasion?"

"You'll see."

At the mountain's peak stood a granite tor surrounded by heathery peat and boulders.

"We're here Jack."

Jack looked around the place. There was no bed, let alone shelter. "What! We're in the middle of nowhere, Cobs!"

"Look again, only this time, cross your eyes."

Jack made a face at Cobs. What was he up to now? But he focused on the tip of his nose until his vision blurred and he could see double. As he did so, the outline of a titanic fortress with towers and turrets pricked the evening skies.

"Ahhhhhh." He should have known to expect the unexpected when he was with Cobs.

The little man nodded. "There are hidden places within hidden places Jack," he said smugly. "Now let's make our entrance."

Cobs approached the granite tor, took off his left shoe, and peeled off a stripy sock. He pointed his stubby great toe at the stack, kicked it once and said,

"Bilberries, damsons,
Grapes from the vine,
Pears and gooseberries,
Ripened through time,
Crab apples,
Cookers,
Eaters and all
Apricots, strawberries,
All fresh for the ball."

Jack couldn't help laughing quietly, and Cobs turned to glare at him. "You'll see," was all he said.

A few seconds passed. Then a small thin branch-like creature poked its head through a crack in the rock and six horse chestnut eyes blinked simultaneously, studying the visitors.

"Come in son of Poitin and son of Matthew. You are honoured guests of my master." It's tone was sarcasatic.

The hairs on the back of Jack's neck stood up. He shuffled behind Cobs, muttering, "How'd he know my father's name?"

"He's The Family Tree, Jack" whispered Cobs. "He can tell everything about you, just by lookin' at you."

They followed the Family Tree past the castle's stone walls, into total darkness.

"Don't be afraid Jack," whispered Cobs, "everything will be fine."

"Afraid? I'm not afraid" retorted Jack. "I'm too busy thinking about what you just said and did to get us in here."

"Oh, the sock thing and Pierce's silly rhyme? He came up with it a very long time ago, and unless you learned it by heart, the miles of journey for the feast would be worthless because they wouldn't let you in."

"What do ya mean worthless?"

"You could come all this way, then queue for hours and Pierce's Ousters protecting the castle would not let you in."

"Pierce's Ousters. What are they?"

"They are a funny breed, stronger than they look and they take great offence at humour. Even my father didn't try to make them smile because if you make them smile, you have deeply offended not only them but also every Ouster they have ever known. They're not a pretty sight when angry, especially on a rare occasion such as this."

"Rare?"

"Oh yes, there used to be a torchlight procession all through the mountains. A sight of wonder. Chains of light linked through the darkness all the way from Tollymore to Pierce Castle's door. That part of the ceremony is gone but others remain. Be warned Jack, if anyone asks you to snatch a burning stick from the bonfire, the trick is to spit on your fingers first, something I learned the hard way."

Cobs turned his hand upwards and held out his index finger and thumb.

"See. No spit means no fingerprints. Anyway, after you've got the stick you put it out in the goody pot."

"Goody pot?"

"My goodness Jack, so many questions."

"I'm sorry." Jack still didn't know what on earth Cobs was talking about. "There's so much to take in."

"No, it's my fault. How should I expect you to know? The goody pot, well, it's..." Cobs closed his eyes for a second, "Mmmmm, bread in hot milk, with sugar and spices, my favourite; cinnamon and black pepper."

Jack was reminded of his mother's bread pudding for a moment and his heart skipped a beat. It wasn't a memory he could share with Cobs.

A dim light came on from overhead, slowly lifting the darkness of the hallway, and Jack could see an ornate mosaic floor beneath his feet. He looked up at the Family Tree with its six branch-like arms, each with six hands, each with six fingers, then jumped as a fanfare of trumpets filled the air. Where was the music coming from? The Family Tree made a grand gesture with all six hands and then announced.

"I give you son of Poitin, the great hunter, maker of dreams, third Lord of Caiserban and bringer of the Nightfall Rainbow. I am proud to announce, Cosabian Broghan Hawsbeard."

The fanfare died to a whimper. The Family Tree took a deep breath, but now he kept his hands by his side and with a tone of distain, he announced: "And here is Jack Turner, an outsider, son of Matthew the fisherman and holder of the secret... the secret... the..."

Jack was finding it hard to hear above the noise of his heart thundering in his ears. What secret? Come on…

But the tree began to cough, as though something had caught in its throat. No matter how hard it tried, it could not clear it. Something was lodged tight. It staggered to one side clutching all of its six hands at its throat and all six eyes blinked, stared and winked at the same time. It leaned heavily against a wall then finally fell to the ground, its branches twisted and broken.

Jack wanted to rush over and put the tree back together again, like Humpty Dumpty. But before he moved a muscle he was aware that all movement in the great hall had stopped, and that all eyes had fallen on him.

Chapter 11
Gifts Bestowed

Jack's cheeks flushed from the burning stares of the gathered crowd and his palms grew clammy. He wiped them on his britches then shoved them into his pockets. He had never felt so nervous in his life. He just wanted to disappear. Then all of a sudden, the crowds began to cheer, jump about, and then cheered some more. From deep within the room came a voice, deep and smouldering.

"Welcome Jack Turner."

As if in a dance, the crowds that stood between Jack and the voice parted opening a clear pathway all the way across the mosaic floor and up to the top of the staircase where Jack stood. He tried to make out what was at the end of the great hall but it was hard, for whatever it was, thick smoke shrouded it. Then, just for a moment, the smoke faded and Jack made out the outline of a man.

But the outline was constantly shifting, transforming from a ball of flame into a block of solid ice, but all the while retaining a human shape. The only thing that didn't alter were the two cold cerulean blue eyes that pierced through the veil of mist.

The deep voice spoke once again. "You have broken The Family Tree, little one. No longer will it be able to tell of my guest's transgressions or see into their family's history and embarrass them by telling secrets that no one should know. I will ask you later how you managed such a feat but for now you are a most honoured guest."

Jack had no idea what had just happened. He was just grateful he wasn't going to be attacked, or taken prisoner. His breathing had just begun to relax when a clap of hands froze the air for an instant. It was followed by the rapturous applause of all the different creatures within the great hall.

"Come! Let the solstice festivities begin."

From the middle of the ceiling hung a great chandelier – Jack had never seen anything like it. Hundreds of candles reflected off thousands of mirrors and their light illuminated huge portraits painted directly on the walls. The faces, all of which looked like they belonged in the past, smiled down at him. Dancers took centre stage, their twirling satin and silk rustling. Three hundred lusty voices sang from choir stalls accompanied by the sound of an exquisite orchestra that resonated overhead. Jack looked up at the circular ceiling and realised that the sounds of the instruments accompanying the choir were coming from metal protrusions that turned and struck the teeth of a steel comb. The room was one giant musical box.

An elaborate fireplace, which must have been about the size of Jack's cottage sat at the end of the great hall and its warmth, filled the room.

Cobs joined Jack at the top of the grand staircase .

"We're in good company Jack," said Cobs.

"Who are they?" asked Jack out of the corner of his mouth.

Cobs began to point out the rooms inhabitants. "Over there in white tie and tails, the ones with the wings like giant dragonflies, they're the Fairies of the Glen; blue blooded royalty. They live within the boundary of the Tree of all Seasons."

"All seasons?"

"Yes, a tree that goes through the four seasons each and every day, and at each day's end it bears a different magical fruit."

Cobs pointed at a group of people in bright dress."They're the Roseroots, over there the Milkworts and the Louseworts." He turned a little further. "Over there are the Tormentils, tooth fixers to those who can afford their skill, and over there – you see the ones with the pointy bright yellow hair? They're the Stag horns." Cobs smiled. "Everyone's here Jack, all the representatives of the kingdom. I see land-crossers and stream-dwellers, sky-bounders and earth-movers. We're in esteemed company. Shall we go and mingle?"

Jack concentrated on walking down the grand staircase without falling, making sure every foot landed on a step. He didn't want to slip and embarrass himself.

"The dance floor," Cobs remarked in a low voice, "it's revolving, so be careful when you step on to it."

The marble floor met the leather of Jack's soles and although he was jostled to the left, he instantly balanced himself. He'd made it. He looked gratefully at Cobs, who grinned back.

Thin hands, green hands, great hands and grimy hands all reached out to greet him. "So pleased to meet you. I'm Lirat."

Jack looked down upon a pale hairless creature and bit the inside of his cheek to stifle a laugh. "Pleased to meet you too." He walked on quickly. He didn't want his hosts to think he was mocking them – but they were a peculiar bunch.

"That was a Drinn," muttered Cobs. "Can you remember how frightened you were of them when you first arrived? Now you can see how ridiculous they are!"

They smiled at one another before yet another hand thrust itself into Jack's face. The Stag Horn bowed, and handed Jack a small wrapped bundle of herbs. "I am Calocera and I wish you to give you a small gift. It is a pouch that holds the spirit of Hartshorn, a great reviver," he said, before making a quick exit.

"Thank you, thank you so very much," Jack shouted to the back of Calocera's head as it disappeared into the jostling crowd.

"At your service," the Staghorn shouted.

"Cobs…"

"Yes Jack."

"What does revive mean?"

"Revive? Well, it means, to restore to life, why?"

"No reason…" said Jack, placing the small bundle carefully into his waistcoat pocket.

Next, a beautiful white haired creature, no taller than Jack's hip and dressed in armour of black leather stood before him. The helmet she wore had wings. "I am Veronica, leader of the Wee Binnians; walkers, dwellers and protectors of the Mourne hills. Take this." She handed Jack a beautiful flower. It had five petals, heart shaped and curved with deep purple veins that grew paler as they reached the thin emerald stalk. "It is a violet Jack, a shrinking violet. Pull a leaf off, and you and the clothes you stand in will become no bigger than my finger. But it only lasts for a short while," said Veronica reaching out her hand.

Jack winced as his knuckles crunched in her stone-like grip. "Thank you very much," he said through gritted teeth.

Cobs ushered him quickly through the room until they stopped by a being no higher than his ankle.

"Ah Jack, this is the mountain conqueror, he travels faster than a heartbeat and has lead many a bewildered soul from their peril. He's held in very high regard across many continents," whispered Cobs.

The creature leapt high into the air, somersaulted twice and landed on Jack's hand. It hopped about, faster than his gaze could follow then halted for an instant, just long enough for Jack to make out a childish face of carved grey stone. A tiny mouth sat beneath two enormous eyes and its forehead ended in a point.

"Let me introduce myself. I'm Bannon, from the Croft of Bar in the City of Yew; a distance from here but I make the journey every solstice. That Family Tree you defeated has always made everyone here uncomfortable, but not any longer and I must thank you for that. Take this. If you ever need my service, just play on it and I'll be there as quick as you can blink. It's only small, so don't go losing it."

Jack took a tiny banjo from Bannon. It was no bigger than his thumb. "Thank you. I'll keep it safe, Bannon." Jack was touched by the little creature's generosity.

Cobs nodded and led him on, pushing Jack forward. It became clear that he was trying to avoid a thin stick-like creature that was trying to catch up with him. But Cobs was unsuccessful. It stopped right in front of them. Jack felt its fusty-damp breath on his face. All eight of its chestnut eyes glared at him.

"You're now my sworn enemy, little one," the creature rasped. "The Family Tree you've so badly injured is my uncle."

"But I didn't do anything," Jack protested. He took a step back, trying to stand tall, pretending he wasn't scared of it.

"That's worse for you. Doing nothing is worse than not doing anything."

"But… but that doesn't even make sense," said Jack trying to sound more confident than he felt.

"The night isn't through with you yet, young upstart." The Family Tree's nephew stuck a leaf-like tongue from the corner of its knotted mouth and drew a thin twig finger across its neck. "I'll be seeing you."

"Not if I see you first you won't," retorted Jack before pushing past him, swiftly followed by Cobs. "Not so friendly now, are they?" Jack muttered to him.

As they moved across the floor, clammy hands, cold hands and many, many more hands reached for the Jack's palm, thanking him, and greeting him, and by the time he and Cobs had reached the far end of the great hall, his fingers were numb.

"Where now?" Jack looked around anxiously. What did this celebration have to do with him? All of a sudden, he felt a very long way from home.

Cobs tugged on his sleeve. "Come with me."

He escorted Jack into a small annex to the side of the great fireplace and pushed him down into a chair. The walls were the colour of soft blue sky and Jack convinced himself that he could see clouds moving across them. He reached out to touch the surface but his hand disappeared and he quickly realised that the walls were actually sky.

"Sit Jack, he'll be with us soon."
"But look, Cobs, you have to see this. These walls aren't real."
"Sit, I said."
Jack slumped into a leather high backed chair, muttering. It had been a long day, and he was weary and edgy. The room suddenly seemed cold and warm at the same time.

"Welcome."

Jack turned his head. A figure was standing there, watching him. Cobs made the introductions. "This is Jack, son of Matthew the fisherman. He has entered our realm in a way nobody else has for nearly a hundred years."

Jack extended his hand in greeting but soon realised Pierce couldn't return the gesture, so he quickly withdrew it.

"I welcome you Jack, son of Matthew the fisherman. I wish to thank you again. No longer to be accountable for our forbears' misdeeds is a freedom we will never take for granted. I must know how you did it."

Jack shook his head. "But I didn't do anything. The tree just fell, that's all."

"That is not all. I built this castle here before I knew what ground it sat upon and that Family Tree's roots worked their way into every fibre of the building, never letting any of us forget our history. That is why everyone here has been so generous and bestowed their precious gifts upon you. They could never have been earned in many a lifetime." He leaned in closer to Jack. "He has familiar eyes, Cobs. I'm sure I've seen them before." He looked for a moment, then shook his head. "Perhaps not. Anyway, you have made a grave enemy tonight, as you now know, so I must ensure your safety whilst you remain under my roof. You will sleep in my Vault. No harm can come to you there but it will not be a comfortable night's sleep and you must be gone by sunrise."

With that, Pierce bowed and left.

Jack watched Cobs stand up and walk towards the wall, before disappearing through it. He remained sitting on his chair and gripped the pillowed seat. After a minute or two Cobs' head reappeared through the wall, floating in a haze of what looked like fog.

"You coming?"
"But…" All of a sudden Jack felt terribly tired.
"You know to trust me by now, come on."
Jack took a deep breath, ran forward, and dived into the wall. He passed straight through it with such speed that he headbutted Cobs hard on the chest, knocking him flying. The little man landed on the iron floor, his head missing a protruding rivet by less than an inch.

Jack was horrified. "Sorry Cobs, you alright?" He rushed over and knelt by his friend.

"I've been better." Cobs fought hard to regain his breath. Apologising again and again, Jack lifted him back onto his feet and dusted him down.

"I'm fine, stop it," he panted. "This is the vault Jack; entirely made of iron... Pierce sleeps here every night... He has to for he's a Samundine, a Prince of the Elements... and he has been in battle with the race of Sylomes ever since he was born."

"What are Sylomes? And what's the fight over?"

Cobs closed his eyes, concentrating on his breathing. Eventually he spoke, his voice having returned to normal. "It's too long to explain now but here is the shortened story. The Sylomes were the first to inhabit this realm. They were the children of earth and sky. Pierce was the first child of water and fire and the two races would not or could not agree on who should be King. A battle raged for thousands of years and Pierce built this room to hide away in when he slept, in order to stay alive. This room remained hidden from the Family Tree and even I cannot explain that. Now come on, it is time for you to get some sleep. I'll be back later to check on you."

"Cobs..."

"Yes Jack..."

Jack took a deep breath. He didn't want to cry. "I'm sorry I haven't thanked you yet for everything you've done for me. You're the first person, apart from my Ma and Da, that believes in me more than I do myself. My Da is the best thing I've ever known and I can't lose him. I know inside he's lost somewhere but I know if I can make my wish come true that he'll return." Tears welled in Jack's eyes. "Cobs, I love him so much. I can't lose him too. We already lost Edmund…"

"I promise Jack, I'll do everything I can to help you. Now get some rest."

Jack undressed and laid his clothes on the chair next to his bed. He reached into the trouser pocket and took out his small broken boat then climbed in to bed and slipped under the bedclothes. He was pleasantly surprised by how comfortable it was. For some reason, he had expected harsh itchy sheets and a mattress made of sharp stones, instead the sheets were silken and the bed contoured perfectly to his body.

He sat the boat onto his chest and rested the broken mast on its deck. He lay listening to his heartbeat, watching the boat slowly rise and fall to the rhythm of his breathing. All the while the party went on outside but he didn't care for such things now.

Was he any nearer finding the way to make his wish come true? The thought rippled through his mind. But, exhausted from the day's events, he welcomed the pillow his head lay upon, and soon his thoughts drifted. He was safe. His eyes shut and soon he was asleep.

A noise jolted Jack from his sleep. It sounded like a branch snapping.

"Who's there?" he shouted, sitting bolt upright in the bed. He looked around. This wasn't the vault where he'd climbed into bed. He was in a small bedroom with a wooden floor and uneven stone walls.

He heard the noise again.

"Who's there?" shouted Jack, shivering.

"Me."

"Me who? Come out and show yourself."

"I told you the night had not yet finished with you, didn't I?"

As if from nowhere the Family Tree's nephew pounced on Jack, its joints cracking with every movement.

Crack!

Two of its branches gripped Jack's wrists, pinning him down onto the bed. He struggled to break free.

Crack!

Two more branches grasped his ankles and a third set of wooden hands grabbed for the pillow, pressing it over Jack's face. He thrashed about beneath the suffocating weight desperately trying to resist the tree's strength.

Crack!

This time the sound came from the centre of Jack's head.

"No..." he cried and sat straight up, sweat soaking the bedclothes. He was back in the vault.

"Are you alright Jack?"

Pierce and Cobs were standing at the end of his bed, their faces showing real concern.

"Good morning, I trust your sleep was troubled," said Pierce.

Jack was still gasping for air. What a strange thing to say. "You're right - I slept terribly," He said finally.

"And the nightmare?" asked Pierce calmly.

"How'd you know?"

"A good guess, I suppose. That and the fact that I've had nightmares every night for as long as I can remember." Pierce sat down on the edge of Jack's bed. "Everything that would have happened last night played out in your dream."

"But it was just a nightmare," said Jack. He was breathing normally now.

"No, Jack. It was as real as I'm speaking to you now, but the vault protected you. I was afraid if you didn't sleep here Death would be your waking friend this morning. This vault has even saved Cobs in the past."

"Pierce!"

"Sorry Cobs. I know you don't like to speak of that time. This vault keeps me alive every night, Jack but it has become my prison. Last night was the first time in over ten thousand sunsets that I have not slept here, but no matter, sunrise is nearly upon us and you must leave. Now!"

Before Jack could take it all in, he was forced to dress in a hurry. He stuffed all the gifts he had received the previous night and his broken boat into his pockets. Then both he and Cobs were quickly ushered out of the gates of the castle.

He looked back over his shoulder and watched as the mighty fortress vanished in the glorious sunrise and only the tors remained. He crossed his eyes but there was no sign of the castle, only the tor that he and Cobs had come upon the evening before.

"What have I done Cobs? Did I offend Pierce?"

Cobs patted Jack's arm. "Not at all, little one, he has saved you from being trapped within the walls of the castle. You see the castle only appears at the summer solstice and won't reappear until the next. Come on, let's be off."

They descended through the castle bogland passing through the mire and reed.

"Over there Jack, that's Batt's wall, it runs by the gap in the winds and the water yonder is called the Fjord of Carling."

Jack looked over the rolling grasslands where the morning sky seemed to rest on the waters surface, its ageless beauty reflecting back into the mountains.

"That's where the Cloc Mor stone rests Jack, where the land meets the water. However, be warned, we're travelling through Trevor's Wood. It is a long trek and once inside don't ever take your eyes off me. Not even for a moment. Do you understand me?"

"No I don't. " Jack inhaled the sea air rising from the distant shore and could smell his father's stories.

"But I'll do anything you tell me Cobs if it gets me what I want."

"Good

Chapter 12
Trevor's Wood

A dense canopy of broadleaved oak trees stood guarding the forest's entrance.

"Listen good Jack. We must keep to the trail in the forest and like I've told ya, don't take your eyes off me for a second. You'll get lost in a flash and there's no way of finding your way out once you do." Cobs shook a knowing finger up at Jack as he spoke. "And by the way don't touch the burning waters from the slopes of this mountain. They drain into a red bog and you wouldn't last long in there I can tell ya."

More orders, thought Jack dropping his head and shrugging his shoulders. *Here we go.*

They pushed their way through some tangled briar and into the wood. The trees' branches swayed and dipped overhead and a red earthen trail reached deep into the undergrowth. Jack didn't take his eyes off Cobs' hat for a moment, after what Cobs had told him he was too scared to. He didn't even let the sounds of chattering squirrels, and wood pigeons distract him, he remained focused.

"Remember Jack......"

"I know, I know," sighed Jack. "Don't take my eyes off you, not even for a second and don't and don't and don't."

Cobs threw a glare towards Jack. "Getting cheeky now are ya?"

"Sorry Cobs."

They trekked deeper into the forest where the light dimmed as the trees thickened.

"We are near the red bog. Stay close."

A branch cracked overhead and startled Jack. He looked up instinctively to where a sparrow hawk was taking flight from high in the trees and in to the sunlight, free of the forest.

"Hey Cobs, did you see that?" said Jack

There was no reply. Jack looked down for an answer but Cobs wasn't there.

"Cobs... Cobs... Where are you?"

His shouts startled a family of field mice and they scurried past him then disappeared down a tiny hole beneath a nearby tree. There was something wrong. Jack looked all around him. The sounds of the forest had stopped. There wasn't a creature to be seen or heard. He would have given anything to hear Cobs voice even if it was nagging him 'not to do this and not to do that.' He had never felt more alone.

The trees seemed to come closer like they were leaning in towards him, examining him. A tingle in his toes distracted him for a moment and he looked down at his boot. It was half submerged in water the colour of rust. Part of the leather upper had been eaten away and his toes wiggled, like they were waving up at him.

The red bog, thought Jack, letting out a desperate laugh. *I don't have long.*

Jack's shoes were wearing thinner and thinner, and no matter how far he tried to distance himself from the acidic waters they just kept seeping towards him, hissing and gurgling, leaving scorched earth in their wake. When his back hit hard against a tree Jack could see no means of escape, and he began to shake uncontrollably. The more he tried to control it the worse it became. His breaths came fast and shallow like a frightened pup. Where was Cobs?

He turned to run but his face hit a wall of bark. He couldn't go left or right for the branches of the trees were woven tightly around each other, trapping him in an unbreakable ring. The thought of the acid eating his body and leaving just a skeleton to be found made him panic even more. The skin on the sole of his foot began to bubble and blister. He hopped onto his tiptoes and stared in dread as the red waters melted his toenails. A sharp pain coursed up his leg and broke his paralysing fright.

What would Cobs do?

Jack dug deep into his waistcoat pocket searching for anything that might help him and first pulled out the small bag of herbs. They were of no use to him. He delved into his pocket for a second time hoping beyond hope that what he was looking for was still there.

Yes! Got it!

Jack held the tiny banjo between his finger and thumb staring at the tiny strings stretched over its frame. Just as he struck a chord, his ankle began to sting horribly. He looked down half expecting to see his shoe being eaten away, but instead the deep dark eyes of Bannon stared back at him.

"Hold out your hand." Bannon kicked Jack's ankle again.

"Bannon," said Jack, his heart lifting at the sight of a friendly face, despite the pain. "You came." He opened his hand and within a heartbeat, the stone hopped up onto it.

"Of course I came. Hey, look Jack," said Bannon pointing to a deep line that ran across Jack's palm. "Do you see this deep line here, well it's is your heart line Jack, it is said to tell how long you are going to live for and it runs on for a while yet so I don't think you're going to die here today."

"That's great, Bannon, and I'm really glad to see you, but could you please tell me how we're going to get out of here? Cobs has vanished, my feet are being eaten away and I can't take any more."

"Get out of here? Sure that's easy. All you have to do is close your eyes."

"What! Close my eyes? But that's how I got myself here in the first place."

"I know it is and it'll be how you get yourself out again. Now if you want my help...?"

Jack nodded and closed his eyes, and Bannon took the banjo and plucked its strings.

"Follow the sound Jack," he said.

Jack limped across gravel and shale, always following the sound, clambering over gullies of what felt like rotting leaves and ice water. Their swampy mixture began to soothe his foot and then, without any warning, the banjo's music stopped.

Jack stood, too afraid to open his eyes. "Bannon, Bannon, are you there?"

"Hmmph you had to look away didn't you? The one thing I told you not to do."

That wasn't Bannon's voice. Jack opened his eyes. Cobs was sat cross-legged and cross-faced on the red path below him.

"It wasn't!" said Jack.

"Wasn't what?"

"The one thing you told me not to do."

"Well, what was the other thing?"

"You told me not to touch the red waters."

"And?" asked Cobs.

Jack held out his boot and his toes poked straight out through the upper.

Cobs took one look, and he couldn't help himself. He fell back into the red earth, holding his sides, laughing, tears running down his rosy cheeks.

"Where's Bannon, Cobs?" Jack asked, embarrassed. Would the wee man ever stop laughing?

"He's a shy creature," replied Cobs finally, trying to stifle his laugh, "not one for pomp, and ceremony is Bannon. He's gone."

"But I didn't get the chance to thank him."

"That's the way he'd want it Jack. He'll know that you're grateful. But he left you this. He told me it was your key."

Jack took the white rose Cobs held out to him, and lifted it to his nose, breathing in its scent. "Key?" he said, puzzled.

"I don't know either, Jack but I think it'd look smart on your cloak. Here, let me help ya." Cobs stood up and Jack bent down so they were at eye level. Cobs placed the rose into one of the holes in the silver brooch.

"Cobs, I just want to say I'm sorry."

"I know. The man that never made a mistake, Jack, never made anything. Now let's be off. I'll mend that shoe of yours later; I'm a dab hand at the cobbling."

They travelled on along the red earthen path for a few more miles. Jack never let the wide brim hat leave his sight, not for an instant.

"We're nearly there, I think," said Cobs eventually. He stopped and looked around, frowning. "I've never been this way before but I'm sure by the distance we've travelled we should be coming out at the top of Slieve Martin. It should be just up ahead." The little man looked puzzled. "But I only see more trees. Something's wrong."

"It's 'cos I got lost isn't it?"

"Nothing of the sort. We can't have gone far wrong. Now stay close."

They had just started walking again when the earth beneath them began to tremble. Jack's gaze shot down to the ground where a single thin root of an oak tree poked through the soil. It rose up at terrific speed and suddenly lashed out at them, whipping the air with a swoosh and a crack.

"Halt!" a voice yelled. "There is no passage here. Go back from whence you came."

"That voice Jack. It's just trying to scare us," said Cobs.

"Well it's worked on me. Let's get out of here."

"No. Stand your ground Jack. This is Trevor's wood and that is Trevor's voice."

Jack's eyes darted from tree to tree until he saw something very strange. The bark on one of the trees seemed to be moving, stretching and twisting, until he could make out the faint outline of something pressing out from the inside of the tree. Then the shape became clear. It was a face made of tree bark with an armoured helmet and a long pointed beard.

Jack mustered up the courage to say, "We just want to pass sir."

The face in tree spoke. "Well no one who has strayed from the path, like you have done, has ever passed this point. What makes you think you shall be the first?"

"I am on a quest sir, a matter of life or death. I will do anything you ask of me but please I beg you, let me travel on."

The nose on the tree-face began to twitch as if sniffing something.

"Come here youthful one, it is my oath that no harm will come to you."

Jack stepped forward to the great oak tree.

"There is a scent upon you?" said Trevor.
Jack breathed in. "Ah. You mean my rose?"
"It is the White Rose of Usher," said the tree warrior, his voice full of sadness and Jack noticed a thin trickle of sap flow from his eye down his face. "She was lost to me centuries ago. Where did you come by your flower, youthful one?"

"It was given to me by a friend." Jack looked at the rose on his cloak then plucked it from his brooch. He held the delicate bud out towards the tree. "Take it sir, it's yours."

The thin root reached out and delicately encircled the thorny stem, then moved it back to the oak warrior. On touching the bark, the rose was slowly absorbed into the tree. "Together again."

Suddenly the trees at the edge of dense forest parted and the bright midday sun shone upon it. Wild grasses and ferns sprouted up and spread rapidly over the barren woodland floor, dotted here and there, by the crimson hue of wild cherries.

"This is our way out Jack," said Cobs in a low voice. "We're within spitting distance. Well you are anyway. Quick, before he changes his mind."

They set off along an overgrown path that ran along the top of the mountain overlooking a vast lough of water with salt marches and mudflats at the edges.

"Look!" shouted Cobs and he set off, tumbling and rolling through the gorse and heather. "Come on, you'll never catch up now."

Jack chased after him, laughing as he bounded down the hillside. Cobs came to a halt and Jack slid to a stop beside him.

"There," said Cobs pointing forward.

"Amazing!" was all Jack could say.

Chapter 13
The Key and the Maze

Jack marvelled at a mammoth rock perched on the hillside. It was taller than his cottage and nearly as long as his father's boat.

"Race you," said Cobs pushing Jack to one side to get a head start.

They dashed towards the rock. Jack gained rapidly on Cobs, then he overtook him.

"I win!" said Jack touching the stone first.

"Woohoo!" shouted Cobs. He leapt into the air then danced a jig. Once he had finished, he explained, "This rock Jack, there's nothing else like it in all of Mourne; in fact in all of Ireland."

Jack raised his eyebrows in disbelief. It was just a large rock, after all.

"Legend has it two giants fought a great battle on this very spot. One of them lifted this rock, heavier than sixty horses, and launched it at his enemy but it landed here high above the Glen of the Faeries and Warren's Point."

"That's some story Cobs but it doesn't really help us any, does it?" said Jack hoping he wouldn't sound too insulting. He pointed towards the distant hills where storm clouds pelted the lands with rods of rain. "And we're gonna get soaked soon so what do you suggest we do now?"

Cobs nodded and took out the parchment from his pocket. He pointed to the writing. "This is the Cloc so vast. The Cloc Mor stone. Now all we have to do is find the lock so small. The rain won't put a stop to that."

"But it could be anywhere."

Cobs began to examine the rock, feeling his way into every nook and cranny. "There has to be a clue here."

"You mean like this here." Jack peered at a name carved into the rock, carved like the name on a gravestone. 'Fulton'," he said, finally. But there are loads more names carved here."

"That's it Jack. The carved names. They must be the creviced scrawls that Erica Tetralix spoke of. They're the names of the Elderfolk, the ones who built the Mourne Wall. Quickly Jack you go and see if you can find the one called Drohan. I'll look here."

Jack went round to the side that overlooked the lough and studied the names carved there, until he came upon the one he sought. His first impulse was to call Cobs but instead he stood staring at the answer to the riddle. He could not help but think of Erica Tetralix. And when he did, he could hear a voice in his mind.

"Touch it."

Gingerly, he placed his finger into the crevice and traced out the letters heavily carved into the stone.

DROHAN

As he reached the end of the letter 'N' the rock began to vibrate, then the ground beneath his feet shook violently.

"What did you do?" Jack heard Cobs yell.

"Nothing! I just followed the outline of Drohan's name with my finger."

"Drohan's creviced scrawl, that's it," said Cobs, appearing from the other side of the rock. "That's the lock, the lock so small. I think you've opened it."

Suddenly a strong wind whipped up out of nowhere and blew furiously around them. Overhead thick storm clouds began to swarm, blocking out the sun.

"I don't like this," said Jack looking up.

"I don't either."

"Can you hear that Cobs?" Jack pressed his ear to rock. "It's coming from inside."

"What is?"

"It's like… steam trying to escape from under the lid of a boiling pot."

Cobs' face fell. "Oh no, I don't think that's steam, Jack. Run! Go on! Run! The rock's gonna blow!"

Jack sprinted down the steep hillside and dived for cover behind an earthen mound, followed quickly by Cobs. They waited. Nothing. Jack couldn't stand it any longer. He peeked over the top and watched the outline of the rock swelling in one place and shrinking in another. Suddenly, a thunderbolt flashed from the storm clouds and struck the mountainside. An explosion of light hit Jack and he ducked back down behind the mound beside Cobs. He shut his eyes and covered his ears as deafening roars erupted from up on the hill. After only a few seconds, there was complete silence. The clouds parted as quickly as they had come and daylight flooded the mountainside once more.

"Come on, it's over, let's get up there," said Cobs, brushing himself down.

"What if it gets struck by lightening again?" replied a worried Jack.

"It won't. The clouds have gone. Come on Jack, are you a Drinn or what?"

Cobs stood up, tucked his fists under his armpits, flapped his bent arms, and made chicken sounds. "Bawk, bawk, bawk."

Jack scowled. "I'm not a coward. I've got this far, haven't I, and nothing's gonna stop me now!"

"That's the spirit," smiled Cobs.

Jack followed the little man up the hill but he kept a good four steps behind him. They neared the great rock again. A charred black line, where the lightening had struck, marked a huge crack and part of the rock lay to one side like a half-hinged door.

Jack dared himself to take a closer look, determined not to let Cobs think he was in the least afraid. He approached the fissure and peered inside.

"Cobs come here. Quick, you've got to see this. The rock's hollow but that's only the half of it."

There was a spiral stairwell in the middle of the hollow rock but when he looked up to where the ceiling should have been, Jack saw the stairway stretching up into a night sky full of bright stars. When he looked towards the rock's base and stairway spiralled down into the earth. It made no sense. Jack smacked his own face- was he dreaming? He stepped back from the rock and looked up into the clear blue sky.

By this time, Cobs had reached him. "Well Jack. You got here first, so the choice is yours. Up or down?"

Jack inhaled deeply. *I'll show Cobs I'm no coward*, he thought, *but going up into nothing is too weird. Down into something, at least I can half understand.* "We'll go down."

They took the crisp granite steps that spiralled down into the bottomless void below but as they descended, Jack kept his head turned towards the shaft of light that came in through the opening in the rock. After ten steps, the light had gone and only darkness and mossy walls lined their twisted descent. Jack began to feel horribly scared and his heart fluttered like a bird but he forced himself to remain calm. He moved with great care holding on to the rock but the corkscrewed journey began to muddle him, he became dizzy and disoriented. He tumbled forward, then down and down for what seemed like forever until he spilled out onto wet cobblestones. A soft glow of purple light surrounded him.

"You alright Jack?" Cobs wasn't far behind.

"What just happened?"

"I don't think you've got the hang of spiral staircases, Jack. I began to feel a bit lightheaded myself back there. Something tells me we've travelled more than just downwards, but where we've ended up I don't know."

"Are we in a cave?"

"Not exactly. It looks like a crystal cavern and by the purple colour I'd say this one is made of amethyst. I've only read of them in one my father's journals but I didn't think they actually existed." Cobs looked entranced by their surroundings.

"You didn't think they actually existed!" said a disgruntled Jack. "A few days ago I thought the archway round my front door was just an archway, now I'm goodness knows how far underground, beneath a giant rock thrown by some legendary giant, in a cave of purple crystal and you're questioning your Da's writings."

Cobs laughed.

Jack got to his feet and looked around. His eyes slowly grew accustomed to the dim purple light and in the distance he could see something flickering. It seemed to rise and fall as if the earth in front of him was moving, almost as if it was breathing.

"It doesn't look like this place holds anything for us, Jack. It's deserted."

"No wait a minute. Can't you see it?"

"See what, Jack?"

"That light."

"There is no light, Jack."

Jack strained to see the candlelight again. There it was, but it wasn't land that it rested upon. He could see a huge stagnant lake covered with a layer of thick dust stretching out into the distance. Jack walked to the lake's edge, bent down, and touched it.

A small release of gas, like air escaping from a porridge pot, carried a tiny wisp of dust into the air and Jack watched as it floated up, higher and higher. The water he had disturbed began to spin, growing larger with each turn and his nose started to twitch as sickening sewer smells erupted from deep under the surface. The filthy water spun into a whirlpool, then rose up into the air, lengthening and expanding. It grew stronger with every turn, stretching from the lake, high up into the cavern until finally it exploded against the ceiling. Fragments of crystal fell down through the vortex of water and flooded the chamber with a dazzling purple brilliance.

A ripple, where Jack had touched the lake spread outwards and as it moved, the ripple grew larger. It swelled into deep concentric circles and the further they travelled from the shore the more powerful they became until they were huge waves, wailing as they churned upwards. Jack's mouth dried up and he stood, scared stiff as a crushing tidal wave raged towards him.

Cobs tugged Jack's arm violently. "Run!"

But Jack didn't budge. He was standing, fixed to the spot. In a single movement, Cobs grabbed him, pulled him down to his eye level then smacked him hard across the face

"Run Jack. Run! Your life depends on it!"

The sting from Cobs' palm on Jack's face brought him back to his senses. He spun round and dashed for the stairwell leaping up the steps, two at a time, racing to get to higher ground. The water surged behind him, licking at his heels. Nearer and nearer, until it trapped Jack in its grip and dragged him downwards. The next thing Jack saw was the cave's wall travelling towards him at lightening speed, and then a terrible pain. Suddenly everything went dark.

"Ahhh!"

"Hold still Jack, you were knocked out."

Jack lay drenched and battered on the cobble floor. He groaned again, but even though he was groggy and sore he forced himself to his feet. They had to get out. The cave glistened now as if washed clean by the flood. He looked back towards the stairwell he'd just tumbled down but it was gone. A wall of solid rock stood in its place.

"There's no way out Cobs!"

"That's the least of our worries Jack. Look out! That wall you're looking at. It's moving towards us."

Jack turned and looked into the cavern for anything that would help their escape. Instead, he stood flabbergasted, pointing his index finger outward. He couldn't speak for he couldn't comprehend what his eyes were seeing. And even if he could, he knew his brain wouldn't believe it. The lake had gone. Different types of fish floundered on the lake floor gasping their last. But the water hadn't evaporated. Oh no. The water had become thick monstrous walls. Yes, monstrous walls of water suspended in thin air. But as if that were not enough, inside these walls swam shoals of fish-like creatures, yellow and red with rows of luminous green teeth that snapped incessantly.

The lake had become one enormous water-labyrinth.

"There's no way back Jack. The only thing we can do now is keep moving forward."

"I can see that," replied Jack curtly, "but I remember my father telling me there was a trick to get out of any maze. You just had to keep your left hand along the left wall when you entered and you'd get to the end. Or at least it would take you back to where you started."

"It would take forever to get to the other side if we tried that and we don't have forever. " Cobs looked around. "I think I might know another way."

Jack watched as Cobs headed straight for the wall of water. Jack's heart was in his mouth as the water hit the little man face on, swallowing him up. Jack began to panic.

This wasn't like when Cobs disappeared into the sky wall in Pierce's castle. This was different. This was water. People drown in water.

"Come back. Don't leave me..." The image of the Caisear Bhan flashed across his mind. "Daaaa!"

Less than a minute later, Cobs walked back out through the wall of water. He was soaked, and Jack could see that the edges of his hat were badly frayed, as though they'd been chewed on.

Cobs looked bright enough though. "It works Jack; we don't have to follow the maze. All we have to do is keep in a straight line and we'll get to the other side in no time. We can hold our breath as we go through the walls of water. I counted to ten to get through the walls but if we run it won't take as long."

Jack couldn't look Cobs in the eye. His head hung low and he traced an arc in the dirt with the tip of his boot.

"What's the matter?" Cobs tried to catch Jack's gaze.

The boy frowned. He was near tears. "I can't do it, Cobs."

"Can't do what?"

"Go with you."

"Why on earth not? Just take a deep breath. It's easy, Jack."

"That's just it. It isn't."

"What do you mean?"

Jack took a deep breath. "Do you remember when I told you my foot was caught in the reeds in Fofanny Dam?"

"Yes."

"Well I lied, it wasn't caught at all. I was drowning. The truth is I can't swim."

"You didn't have to lie; many a fisherman can't swim, Jack."

"I know that, but…"

"But what?"

"It's not easy to explain…"

"Go on, try."

Jack's shoulders began to shake. He felt ashamed. "Do you want the truth?"

"Yes Jack, go on."

"I'm scared of the water Cobs. I mean really scared, petrified in fact."

Cobs gulped. He gazed up at Jack, his eyes full of concern.

"There, are you happy now. I'm scared of water! Ever since my brother… It's why I could never go out fishing with my Da. I know I'm a disappointment to him. He told me once that we all have a fear inside of us and that the lucky ones get the chance to overcome it." Jack lifted his head a fraction. "He told me I was lucky."

Cobs nodded slowly. "From what you've told me Jack, it's no wonder you've such a fear and it's certainly nothing to be ashamed of. And from what I've seen of you so far, you could never be a disappointment to anyone, especially not your father. Now Jack, I want you to close your eyes, take a deep breath in and hold it."

"Why?"

"Now's not the time for questions. Just trust me and do it."

Jack closed his eyes.

"You see, it's easy. For a start, you don't need to know how to swim and as for the water, you are walking through it not diving into it." Cobs could see the wall closing in behind Jack, but his voice remained calm. "Now count to ten."

Jack counted and with every passing number, Cobs watched the wall creeping two steps closer.

"That's all there is to it Jack. See you've done it. There's no difference holding your breath out here in the air than there is inside the walls of water. The fact is you can do it. If you want, I'll take you by the hand. Do you think you can do it?"

"No I can't, alright. I just can't. It's easy for you."

"The way I see it Jack you've no choice. Open your eyes."

Cobs turned Jack around and he could see the wall of rock fast approaching.

"If you stay here you'll be crushed to death. Now come on, I'll be there with you."

"Are you sure?"

"Yes I'm sure."

"Well if you're with me, then I think I can. I never wanted to let my Da down, you see…"

"You could never do that."

"Thanks Cobs."

"Alright then, let's go."

The instant Jack and Cobs stepped onto the boggy lake floor together they no longer had control of the direction they were going. They skidded across the treacherous surface and all the while, they grabbed at one another trying to stop themselves from falling. By the time they reached the water labyrinth, the granite wall had already reached the edge of the lake.

Jack took a deep breath, grabbed Cobs by the hand, and squeezed it hard. He counted frantically and reached the number ten much quicker than Cobs. When he opened his eyes, he expected to be in the first of the labyrinth's many pathways, but instead he was still under water, surrounded by hundreds of snapping jaws. A hundred fish with mouths filled with a thousand sharp teeth were poised to attack him. The shock made him gasp.

Stinging salt water surged through Jack's nostrils, travelling at lightening speed to his lungs. He tugged hard on Cobs arm trying to get his attention but Cobs tugged just as hard back. A second later, they were through the first wall. Cobs turned and watched as Jack coughed, spluttered, and spat out mouthful after mouthful of the lake water, struggling for breath.

"I don't mean to rush you, Jack but I'm afraid we must hurry, time is against us. Look!"

Jack turned to see the granite wall pushing its way through the maze.

"But those fish ..."

"Don't think about them. Come on, it can't be far now."

They crashed into wall after wall of water, always a few steps ahead of the stone wall. Jack closed his eyes every time he became immersed and only saw fleeting flashes of light when he entered the pathways, gasping for air. Faster and faster they ran, never looking back until they burst through the other side of each wall and Jack could inhale deeply for a moment. He closed his eyes waiting for the next soaking but Cobs gave his sleeve a tug.

"Look. We made it," he said.

They clambered up the lakeside, until they could climb no higher and were perched on a crystalline precipice. Jack threw a glance over his shoulder but all he could see in front of him was a mass of grey. Now he could feel his ribs ache as the crushing weight of the granite wall pressed against him. He was pinned down with no hope of escape.

A voice like an avalanche rumbled out across the chamber.

"Cease!"

Cobs and Jack were squeezed so tight they couldn't move even if they wanted to so the command had no effect on them. But much to their relief they quickly realised whoever it was shouting had not intended the order for them. They breathed a sigh of relief as the crushing weight of the wall released them as it began to retreat.

"Whoever is up there, thank you," shouted Jack.

A head appeared and an arm stretched out and pulled each one of them up onto a shelf of rock. Jack found himself staring into the face of an old man. No, not old, this was an ancient face. Deep lines, etched by the hand of time, ran across his forehead. A full grey beard flowed from his chin and his nose hooked downwards as if it were chasing after it. Over its hunched back lay a purple cloak of moth-eaten velvet and beneath it, a long green robe laced with a golden rope tied around the middle.

"You came little one. Thank you," he said in a tired whisper. His mighty command for the wall to stop seemed to have drained all the strength from him. "I am Nieron. I have been trapped here since the day of the great battle. When I tried to go back to the surface I could not, for a great weight of granite blocked me."

"But how come you didn't die?"

"The remaining energy from the Cloc Mor stone has fed the crystal walls of this cave and they in turn have kept me alive and taught me many of its secrets. Now you have come I can finally leave and return to my birthplace to seek out my kin."

"But the wall of granite?" asked Jack, glad to see it gone.

"It has receded and the steps to the outside are once again open."

"Then let's go."

"I have waited this long, a few more moments will make no difference. I'm puzzled, young one. Only a true believer could open the lock and you have done that, but to free the waters of the lake, that is a gift even I cannot explain."

"I just touched them, that's all."

"That is not all. You must be rewarded. I have three gifts for you. I wish to light your path, give you the gift of persuasion but most of all, the power of prophecy."

Nieron continued to speak to Jack but Cobs showed no interest in their conversation, instead he clambered around on his knees brushing up all the long stray hairs shed from the Drewron's beard. He stuffed handful upon handful into his backpack until he could fill it no more.

"Take this. Once it is lit, it will never go out," Nieron said handing Jack a small candle and then he explained the unusual way to light it.

"And take this also."

He handed Jack a small leather pouch. "It is filled with sand that once thrown into the air, takes a long time to fall. As it descends anyone within earshot will listen to your every word and believe it to be true."

"Thank you sir," said Jack bowing his head.

"Now my third and final gift is the most precious. It is an incantation. But you must not interrupt me once it starts."

"I promise," said Jack.

Nieron closed his eyes and opened his mouth wide. Voices poured from deep within him, ringing out like flawless crystal.

> "Follow the Rare Ring Ouzel,
> As its wing takes flight o'er the wall,
> Beneath the Bellmouth's Pillar,
> Where youthful teardrops fall."

The Drewron opened his eyes and stared at Jack.

"That incantation has never been sung before. Never speak aloud what I have told you. It must never come from your mouth but once it is told then you can speak of it."

Jack looked at the creature, utterly confused.

"You are so very special young one and a great deal is ahead of you, but we must leave this place now."

The three of them walked back through the great maze of water and left the cavern by the spiral stairs. As soon as the Drewron reached the daylight, he flinched as though in pain. The evening sunlight seeped through the many folds of his cloth warming his skin.

"I thought I would never feel the sun on my face again. Thank you Jack."

Nieron faced the great rock of Cloc Mor and touched it with an open palm. The doorway closed but a scar remained upon the rock from where it had been.

"I am free now; I have my life to go back to."

"But what about us? Where do we go from here? You have given me a prophecy but sworn me never to speak it out loud, and I haven't a clue what it means."

The Drewron just walked off. He didn't even look back, instead just shouted "You're a smart pair. You'll find a way."

"Don't worry Jack," said Cobs. "If it's a prophecy that needs to be unravelled I will introduce you to a very old friend of mine. She's bound to help and she lives on the slopes not far from here."

Chapter 14
Premonition Untold

Jack and Cobs travelled on until they reached an ancient burial mound, high up in the hills and from its vantage point, they could see for miles.

"Do you see that castle down there Jack?"

"The one with the huge wall all the way round it?"

"Yes. That is Darnas, the animal sorcerer's castle. It means we are nearly there." Cobs shouted out, "First Sister of the Heather, Mother to the Southern Shores and oldest friend of the Clan Hawksbeard I need you."

Jack could hear scraping and grinding as a small stack of rocks rolled over one another, moving towards him from the burial mound. From its centre rose a single pink blossom that stretched and bent as it lifted its head from the soil. Jack could not believe what he was seeing; another lady was emerging from the ground and she looked just like Erica Tetralix, except she wore a deep pink gown and her crown was of golden pollen grains that glistened in the sun's dying rays. She stood slightly taller than her sister did.

"Jack, let me introduce you," said Cobs proudly. "This is Erica Ling, the First Sister of the Heather. Someone I've known even before I first crawled.

"I am pleased to meet you Jack. And as always Cobs, it is a pleasure to see you."

Cobs bowed and removed his hat as he did so.

"I know why you've come. Follow me," said Erica. They walked for another mile until Erica stopped. "This is the Chamber of Kilfeaghan, the mighty chieftain; we can rest here for the night and talk of times past."

The three of them settled around a small but welcoming fire under a sloped roof of rock. Cobs sat cross-legged and removed the long hairs of the Drewron's beard from his sack. He began to roll them, licking his fingers, joining one strand to another. All the while Jack listened intently to Ling's tales of Cobs' youth.

"My favourite memory of Cobs happened nearly a hundred years ago when he was no bigger than he is now," laughed Ling. "He helped catch all the dandelion clocks of a young girl from the Outer Realm and helped make her wish come true but like all youngsters he didn't listen to the whole wish. He missed a part... Not the sort of thing a mother in the Outer Realm really wants to see."

"What?" asked Jack looking at Cobs.
"Her daughter floating above the house," said Erica.
Jack could not help but laugh. "My birthday wish was better than that, Ling. I waited a whole year for it but then I had to change it..." His laughing stopped and his voice dropped. "It still didn't come true though...."

"Things don't always happen for a reason Jack," said Ling, "and when they do, it is sometimes hard to understand what that reason is. Isn't that right Cobs?"

Cobs could no longer hear the conversation; the mention of the girl who could fly took him into a world of his own.

"Cobs! Cobs!" said Ling. "Are you with us?"

He shook his head. "Sorry. I was miles away, thinking of a young girl in a cream dress with a pink ribbon around her waist hiding behind the petticoats of her older sister… Anyway, enough of that, where were we? Ah yes… food… I'm starving. I'm so hungry I could eat the southbound end of a northbound pig."

Ling waved the long sleeve of her gown over a flat rock table and when she removed it, the bounty of the forest lay ready for feasting. Carved wooden bowls overflowing with grapes and berries nestled next to huge silver platters filled to bursting with plump damsons, orchard apples, and juicy ripe pears. Golden cups were filled to the neck with a delicious honey and cinnamon liquid. Jack and Cobs drank their fill and ate 'til bursting.

"My Ma would love you Ling," said Jack with a mouth stained with berry juice and a black tongue to match.

Cobs laughed, "Yes so would many a mother, my own…" He stopped mid flow.

"Cobs." Ling's tone showed concern.

"I know, I know," replied Cobs. "But now's not the time Ling." Cobs turned to Jack and placed a hand on his shoulder. "Jack, tell Ling what the Drewron told you."

"I can't Cobs, I swore not to tell it aloud."

"You can tell me," said Ling gently but emphatically, this time her lips did not move. Her voice spoke directly to Jack's mind.

"Can you hear me?" thought Jack.

"Yes I can hear you. Now what do you have to tell me?"

Jack explained how he freed the Silver Bearded Drewron and of the prophesy about the Rare Ring Ouzel, the Great Wall and the Bellmouth.

"I can now tell Cobs what you have told me. I will not speak aloud so your promise will still be kept."

Ling looked from Cobs to Jack and back again. They could both hear her in their minds.

"You have been told of a legend that I thought untrue. It tells of the Rare Ring Ouzel, one of Ireland's rarest birds. Tiny blackbirds with a distinctive band of bright white plumage across their chests, they had a sound so melodic and full of sadness it mesmerised anyone within earshot. The wall the Drewron speaks of is the Mourne Wall for nothing can fly over it. As for the Bellmouth and the teardrops, I know nothing of them."

"I still don't understand Ling," thought Jack

"I do Jack," said Cobs. His mouth did not move for Erica had linked all their minds together.

"The Rare Ring Ouzel lived in the uplands and blanket bogs of Slieve Donard," said Cobs.

"Cobs," interrupted Ling, "the Rare Ring Ousel needed the mature heather to live on. But Erica Cinera, the Third Sister of the Heather, disappeared off Donard Mountain nearly a hundred years ago and neither she nor the bird have been seen since."

"It's all we've got to go on. We must travel on to Slieve Donard."

"But Cobs, you can only go by way of The Wall. The rest of the premonition cannot come true if you do not," explained Ling.

A gurgling sound from Jack's stomach broke the silent conversation.

"Excuse me," said Jack, "I think I ate too much."

The talking went on into the small hours until one by one, eyes grew heavy, heads weary, and soon everyone was asleep.

Chapter 15
The Drewron's Rope

The next morning Jack awoke and without a word, got up and left the tiny shelter. He walked barefoot through the dewy grass to get a better view of the sea. He had heard the waves crashing against the shore the previous night so he knew it was close. The first flickers of light played on the water's surface and out on the mudflats he could see small creatures foraging.

"Jack! Breakfast's ready. Do you hear me? Now come and get it before it gets hot."

Jack smiled at Cobs laughing at his own joke. "Coming!" he shouted but he hesitated, not wanting to leave the scene before him.

After a few minutes Cobs shouted again." Did you hear me? Now hurry up, Ling has already gone, and we've to get going soon too."

Jack trudged back to Cobs, muttering under his breath. He sat at the stone table and ate his breakfast in silence, huffing for being summoned like a child. Cobs took something from his backpack and threw it towards Jack, catching him unawares.

"Get it off me, get it off me," said Jack, his hands frantically flying across his cheeks.

"Calm down Jack and look out of the corner of your eye."

Jack looked down, and there on his cheek lay a thin cord. He pinched it between his finger and thumb then followed its length right back to Cobs' hand.

"What is it?" asked Jack.

"A rope."

"What?"

"You heard. A rope."

"What'd you throw it at me for?" said a disgruntled Jack.

"I was trying to catch that bad mood of yours that's all," Cobs said smiling. "I'm sorry for calling you like that earlier. It's just when I woke up and you weren't there I got a bit worried."

Jack couldn't help but return the smile.

"Sorry for wandering off," apologised Jack. "So where'd you get the rope anyway?"

"That creature under Cloc Mor Stone was a Silver Bearded Drewron. They're a secretive people from the dark woods of Thunders Hill. While you and Ling were talking I collected all the hairs the Drewron had shed and wove three ropes out of them."

Jack examined the rope, unable to see where one strand finished and the other began.

"Once the strands are woven together they can never be broken," said Cobs. "The rope is unbreakable." He wound it loosely around his open hand and placed it back into his backpack along with the two others he had made. Then he lifted the rest of the fruit spread out on the stone table and shoved it all in the bag as well.

"Waste not, want not… Now let's be off, we've a long day ahead of us."

Jack pulled on his boots and wriggled his toes expecting to see them poking through the upper but he couldn't.

"Hey, you mended them. Thanks," beamed Jack.

"Have awl will travel," laughed Cobs.

They set off down the mountain into a willow-green valley lined with tall fir trees and a river of white foam coursed through its centre.

"That's Knockchree just yonder," said Cobs pointing to a tiny hill, "I'd love to show you the flying Hawk Rocks in the old quarry there, but we don't have the time."

"What are they anyway?"

"Rocks that are lighter than air and can fly you anywhere just by asking."

"Then why don't we ask them?"

Cobs stuttered and quickly looked down at his boots. "…Because we have a path we must follow. The Drewron has given his prophecy and we must keep true to it."

"I still don't see why we can't ask the rocks."

"We just can't!" came a defiant reply.

"Why not?"

"If you really want to know it's because…"

"Yes," said Jack.

"I'm…"

"Yes."

"I'm afraid of flying. There I've said it. I fell off a Hawk Rock once as a child and I promised myself I'd never get on the back of another one."

"So the Drewron prophecy?" probed Jack.

"Alright, getting on a rock won't break the prophecy. You can fly on ahead if you want, but you're on your own."

"Nah! I'd better stick with you. Knowing my luck I'd fall off a flying rock and land in a lake."

Cobs laughed.

They passed on through a village of tiny houses with beach-pebble walls and hazel thatch roofs. Jack could see the lace curtains twitch in every window but not a creature came outdoors to greet them.

A thick mist began to descend but Jack and Cobs travelled on.

"I'm afraid from here on Jack, our journey really begins."

Chapter 16
Wall and Silver Orb

Jack shivered in the cold mountain air for the sun's warm rays were blocked by the mist. It swirled around him until he could see no further than the length of his arm. He hunched his shoulders and pulled his cloak up tighter around him.

"We're lost."

"Never Jack! Not as long as I have this."

Cobs reached into his waistcoat and took out his pocket watch. The golden case glowed in his hand and Jack could clearly see the raised outline of the Hawksbeard crest. He watched as Cobs pressed on the winder and the cover sprang open to reveal a dial with four quarters, each one depicting a different season. Even though Jack had only seen a few watches in his life, he knew this one wasn't ordinary. Cobs pressed the winder again and this time, the face of the watch sprang up and beneath it lay a compass. Jack gasped.

"Get the map in my backpack. It's a long rolled up piece of cloth. Looks like a Drinn's chewed on it."

Jack untied the pack and lifted out a tattered piece of parchment.

"Here ya go," and he handed the map to Cobs.

"No Jack, you open it."

Jack unrolled it. On the top left corner sat a red wax stamp of the Hawksbeard crest, with north, south, west, and east marked clearly. The map had all the names of the mountains except for a section where a huge chunk of detail was missing.

"It's a map of the Mournes, Jack."

Cobs sat the compass onto the map and Jack stared intently as a tiny quivering light skipped from the winder across to the parchment. It stretched outwards and illuminated every outline drawn on the paper.

"That's amazing. Where'd you get it?"

"My father gave me the compass-watch on my two hundredth birthday. I only had to wait another fifty years for him to give me the map though," laughed Cobs.

Jack noticed a single spot of red light on the map.

"What's that Cobs?"

"The red spot is where we're standing right now. I told you we weren't lost."

"But that's incredible. How does it work?" said Jack looking under the map for any clues.

"I have no idea. My father said a Smew was able to get it for him but not to ask anything more than that."

"But tell me, what's that thick black line there, Cobs?" asked Jack, pointing to the centre of the map. "There are names of places, rivers, and mountains but nothing inside of that line. It's as if the map wasn't finished."

"That thick black line's where we're heading," Cobs replied, his tone becoming more serious. Jack knew better than to ask any more questions.

They headed up to the mountain peak through the thickening blanket of fog. Jack noticed that the red dot on the map moved as well, as though following them.

In the distance, Jack could see something looming out of the mist. As he drew nearer, he could see an immense dry stone wall, rising up like granite armour. It ran in a ribbon along the length of the hills as far as his eyes could see, draped in moss and lichen, looking as though it had withstood the elements for thousands of years.

"This is the mighty Mourne Wall Jack. We have to climb up onto it and walk its length until we reach Slieve Donard. It's where Erica said we'd find the Ousel bird."

Jack could see no way to scale the wall and he didn't like the thought of being up that high anyway.

"Why can't we just walk along side it? It's quite a drop from up there!"

"The Drewron said we must look for the Rare Ring Ouzel as it flies over the wall and for that reason we have to walk on top of it."

"I don't understand."

Cobs stared at him. "That's just it Jack, you don't understand. This is no ordinary wall. It has been here forever and it protects us. Nothing can fly over it. Nothing ever has and nothing ever will!"

To prove his point Cobs lifted a stone, aimed it above the wall and threw. Jack watched, envious of Cobs' pitching arm as the stone flew high into the air, and he stood in disbelief when the stone bounced back towards them.

"What the…?"

"You try Jack."

Jack lifted a stone and threw it. He watched as it lifted into the air and he waited for it to disappear from view over the wall, but it didn't. Instead, it cleared the top of the wall, stopped for a fraction of a second then bounced back and hit him square on the chest. He was sure that when the stone had stopped in mid air he could see something shimmering around it, but only for a brief moment.

"We've got to get onto the wall Jack."

Cobs walked along the wall's edge until he came to a wooden stile with slippery green rungs. He ushered Jack up them and he followed onto the wall's back.

"Try to put your hand over the other side of the wall."

Jack reached outwards and as he did, the tiny hairs on the back of his arm rose up. Then the wool of his cape stood up too and began to crackle. He moved his hand a little further forward until suddenly an invisible force, as cold as ice pressed back against his palm and froze it to the spot. He instinctively tried to pull it back but it was stuck fast. He couldn't shift it no matter how hard he tried.

Jack was beginning to panic when, without warning, a streak of bright blue light shot down from above him and raced towards his open palm. The instant it made contact with his hand five brilliant streams of light erupted from his fingertips up into the evening sky. Jack could see that the lights travelled in one direction. Not like the normal fireworks that he had seen at Halloween, the ones that exploded in the air and went in every direction. This light looked almost as if were trapped between two sheets of glass. When the streams of light reached their pinnacle, a tremendous rumbling ripped through the air and a dazzling explosion knocked him clean off his feet.

"Oooowww!!!…. Jack screamed. "What the heck was that?"

"That…"

"Yes that…"

"Oh. That was the Silver Orb."

Chapter 17
The Shimnavore

Cobs helped Jack to his feet and dusted him off.

"You've just been struck by Orb lightening, but you'll be all right."

Cobs took Jack's clenched fist and forced it open. Hundreds of tiny blue sparks ran inside the spiral grooves of his fingertips then flowed down onto his palm and fizzled out.

"Told you it was no ordinary wall didn't I? This is the Mourne Wall. She runs in a near-circle over fifteen of the highest peaks and deepest valleys. The Silver Orb travels with her. The Orb is a giant bubble of energy that covers everything within the boundary of the wall. For thousands of years, no creature has breached it; not from the air, not even from underground."

"You mean there's no way in or out?" said Jack in disbelief.

"That's right. Nothing can enter and nothing can leave but I wanted you to see it with your own eyes."

"Tell me more Cobs."

"There's nothing more to tell."

Cobs held Jack's eyes with a stern gaze.

"Do you see what you've gotten yourself into? I told you the day we met you could've gone home, but you chose to follow me. I only hope you were right."

Jack didn't choose to follow Cobs – he chose not to give up the search for the answer.

"Course I was right. It's the only chance I have of making my wish come true. I'll face death itself if it means bringing my father home!"

"That may well happen. Now come on."

They walked carefully along the wall as it rose steeply along the rugged slopes of Binnian Mountain. After a short distance, a sheer face of granite rock forced them to stop.

"The wall's disappeared Cobs."

"No it hasn't Jack, it goes straight through the rock, but we can't follow it. We'll have to meet it on the other side"

They drifted to the right of the wall and headed for a notch high in the top of the mountain, holding on tightly to the huge Tors, taking great care not to slip. When they met the wall again, on the other side, an amazing panoramic view left Jack speechless.

Cobs pointed out all he could see. "Way out there, in the distance, are the hills of Dyflin, and beyond are the Mountains of the Toothless One, where the Norse race still roams."

The north wind blew hard, lifting the cape from Jack's shoulders but he did't feel it, for he was too in awe of the scenery that surrounded him. He turned round and he gazed, inward, beyond the wall, beyond the Orb. He stared in wonder at a huge lake where dark human-like shapes were leaping high into the air before disappearing back into the depths.

"Did you see that Cobs? Something's in that lake down there, inside the wall. What are they?"

"I'm sorry Jack I can't tell you."

"Why not?" said a disgruntled Jack.

"It's not that I won't tell you. It's that I can't tell you. No one can. Nothing is known of the Inner Realm."

"The Inner Realm?"

"Yes, beyond the wall. There are three realms. You are from the Outer Realm, the land of humankind. I am from the InBetween, the jewel of all nature but everything inside the Mourne Wall is known as the Inner Realm, a place long forgotten."

Cobs quickly changed the subject.

"Jack, I forgot to say to you, look down there," he turned his back on the Inner Realm and pointed, "that's Carrick Little Mountain and just beyond it, is Annalong."

"Hey, that's where I'm from," said Jack excitedly. "Can you see my house from here?"

"Only if you sneeze, Jack or if you accidentally find yourself daydreaming."

"What?"

"When you sneeze or when your mind wanders, when you are in the InBetween, the True Kingdom of Mourne, you sometimes catch a fleeting glimpse of your realm. I've seen its carved paths and dwellings a plenty. It works the same from your side."

Jack frowned. "Hey, it's strange you say that. I remember once I was in my garden when I was looking towards Carrick Little Mountain and I could have sworn I saw something weird. Definitely not from my realm, as you put it. But it was gone in a flash."

"What did it look like?"

"I don't know, but I do remember one thing though. It moved awkwardly, as if it was running backwards. I can't explain it any better than that but all I know is that a terrible chill ran down the length of my spine. I'd never felt anything like it before, or since for that matter."

"A chill!" shrieked Cobs.

Jack took a step back from him.

"What does a boy know of a chill?"

"Nothing!" replied Jack, surprised by Cobs' angry tone. "When Nanna Tess got a chill down her spine she said it was someone walking over her grave. I never understood what she meant 'til that day."

"And what day was it?"
"I can't remember."
"Think boy!"
"It was... Oh, I know... the day it snowed on my house. The day I made my first wish. My tenth birthday. Why?"

"No reason Jack. No reason," replied Cobs, his tone easing.

Jack had the feeling he'd said something he shouldn't. "What's the matter Cobs? Have I done something wrong?"
"No."

"Then why are you so mad?"

"I'm sorry, I shouldn't have snapped at you. It's just there's something in my father's notes that tells of a chill and soon after it... well never mind, it's just a silly poem."

"Tell it to me."

"No!" said Cobs emphatically.

"Doesn't end well Cobs, does it?"

"Enough of this nonsense, we've a way to go before nightfall. I know a place to shelter, now come on."

The wall seemed to shrink as it descended the mountain and through a forest of larch trees that lined the banks of a fast flowing river.

Cobs kept up a running commentary as the walked. "That's Annalong Wood. It's a ..."

Jack turned to see why Cobs had stopped.

"What is it?" The little man was as white as a sheet.

"Ssssshhhhh! Can't you smell it?" Cobs sniffed the air, his nostrils twitching trying to hone in on the scent. He spun round and pointed straight into the Inner Realm.

"That smell's coming from in there. I'd know it anywhere."

Jack looked in the direction of Cobs' finger and an icy cold shiver ran down his spine.

"Get down!" said Cobs as he grabbed Jack by the scruff of his cape and dragged his face down to meet the wall's bare rock. "That can't be!"

Jack could hear branches crack and the trample of hooves in the distance. Even with the side of his face pressed against the cold stone, he could see the trees, inside the Inner Realm, falling, one by one. Something thrashed through the tangled undergrowth then stepped out through a break in the forest. Jack's eyes nearly popped out of their sockets.

A creature, bigger than any horse he had ever seen, rose up on two powerful hind legs, a cavernous ribcage sat upon a deeply retracted abdomen. Then its neck extended from massive shoulders that supported an oversized skull and a long muzzle that bore jagged fangs, dripping with thick frothing saliva. It jerked from left to right and sniffed the air, nostrils flaring. The hair on its head writhed with a life, all its own, each coarse strand weaving around the other trying to beat off a greedy wave of swarming flies. A mighty tail curved to the ground, the tip, ending in a razor-sharp trident fork and on every joint of its body, a sharp serrated thorn sprouted.

The weak evening sunlight struck its scaly skin instantly blistering it, sending an acrid stench, like burnt seaweed, high into the air. Thick greasy fumes caught the back of Jack's throat and he clasped his hand over his mouth, to stop himself from being sick.

When Jack turned to Cobs he could tell that he too was horrified by what he saw.

"I can't believe it," Cobs whispered. "It's not possible. That creature's extinct; wiped from the face of this, and every realm, long before my kind was even born."

"What is it Cobs?"

"A Shimnavore!"

Chapter 18
The Holocene

Something glowed in the Shimnavore's fist but Jack couldn't make out what it was. He leaned in closer towards the Orb. Although it was invisible, he knew it was there and he knew the consequences of touching it. Another wave of the foul stink hit him making him cough. The Shimnavore stopped in its tracks, hair erect. It didn't turn around to see what made the noise, it didn't need to, for Jack could see two unearthly yellowed eyeballs staring right out from the back of its head. He froze, breathless, praying he would go unnoticed. The creature looked right in his direction but it mustn't have seen him for it just shook its head and moved on.

"It didn't see me Cobs," said Jack letting out a relieved sigh.

"Thank goodness."

"I've seen it before you know!"

"Don't be stupid Jack. That's impossible."

"Don't call me stupid," an angry Jack replied, "I have seen it before. It moves in the same way and I got that chill again, same as on my tenth birthday. It's massive Cobs, must be three times as big as a wolfhound."

"Don't be fooled by size alone. It's even more deadly than that. The Shimnavore were originally bred as War-Dogs by the Ancients to fight for them and they brought down every army they were sent up against. But the

Shimnavore grew smart and more powerful with every kill, until finally they turned on their masters and in one night they wiped them out. But then came the Holocene and all the Shimnavore vanished."

"What was the Holocene?"

"A war. The greatest of wars. When good finally overcame evil. But I'm afraid I can't tell you any more than that, for it is all anyone knows."

"Did you see something glowing in its claws?"

"Yes I did Jack. I'm afraid that's frightened me even more than seeing the beast itself. That's what I could smell. Those things in its claws were dandelion clocks!"

"Clocks!" said Jack in shock. In his mind, he could see his jar back on the stairs in the Curraghard tree and his wish for his father's return waiting to come true. "You mean the Shimnavore's the one that's been stealing them?"

"It has to be. But I don't understand it. Nothing can break free of the Wall Jack. Dandelion clocks don't grow in there and they can't enter either."

"So how did it get them?"

"I don't know Jack, but for you to have seen the Shimnavore from the Outer Realm it can only mean one thing but it's impossible. The Shimnavore must have been in the InBetween."

"We have to follow it Cobs. That thing has the stolen clocks that could make my wish come true."

"Follow it. Are you mad? For a start, it's inside the wall and we can't go in after it. Even if we could there's something else I haven't told you."

"What?"

"It was said that one touch of the Shimnavore's skin would make you age a hundred years…" Cobs clapped his hands together, "…in an instant! Anyway, we can't leave the capstones. The Wall will know we've gone and then the Drewron's prophecy….."

"I don't care about his prophecy!"

"Don't be too hasty Jack. It's the only reason we've got this far and it might be the only thing that gets you what you want. Besides, it's late now, we have to get some rest."

Their shadows stretched out before them as the sun set beyond the western shores. Intense hues of burnt orange reached across the clouds making the wall appear as though it were on fire. But the air soon grew cool and they quickly realised they were in for a long night on the exposed hills.

"We need to make camp just beyond here Jack. It's more sheltered."

"We're not camping on the wall are we?"

"Yes we are. I know a place not far from here. Come on."

The wall rose to a great height and Jack's steps grew more wary as he strained to climb it. Cobs came to an abrupt halt and Jack walked straight into the back of him.

"What's the matter?"

"Look Jack. Part of the wall has fallen away. It's impossible to get to the other side."

"There's no going back Cobs. Why can't we just climb down?"

"It's too dangerous. You saw what happened when you touched the Orb, can you imagine if you slipped and fell against it. You'd be killed."

Cobs sat down and crossed his legs, with his eyes closed. He began to hum to himself, quietly at first but with each passing minute, he got louder and louder until his eyes popped open and he sprang up.

"I've got it! How strong do you think you are Jack?"

"I don't know, why?"

Cobs explained his plan then removed his backpack. He opened it and unravelled something from inside.

"I'm ready now Jack."

"I really don't like this."

"Just remember Jack, on my count."

"The count of three?"

"Three! Three! What a waste o' time. We always go on the count of one."

"One! No one goes on the count of one."

"Alright Jack, there's no point fighting over it now. Saying as you're the one doing it, three it is."

Jack reached down and strained as he lifted Cobs by the left ankle. He hung like a rag doll in his grip.

"You can do it," said Cobs, the blood rushing to his head. Jack started to spin round, picking up speed. Cobs felt heavier with every turn.

"One, two, threeeeee…!"

Jack let go and Cobs flew off into the night. Within a few seconds, Jack could hear a thud, then nothing.

"Cobs! Cobs! Are you alright?"

There was no reply.

"Cobs, are you alright?"

The silence continued for another minute until a faint gravely voice coughed.

"I think so. The rocks broke my fall."

Jack laughed.

"Have you got hold of your end of the rope?"

"Yes," replied Jack.

He tied his end to a large stone anchored in the wall and Cobs did the same on his side.

"Well come on Jack. What's keeping you?"

Jack's hands trembled. "How do you know it won't break?"

"It's the rope from the hair of the Silver Bearded Drewron. It can't break. For goodness sake, I did the hard bit tying it to my leg and getting' chucked over here. Now hurry."

Jack tested the rope and it held. He hooked one foot over the rope, and let the other one hang to balance himself. He began to move hand over hand, pulling himself slowly along the length of the rope. After a minute or so, he looked down and found he was hanging high over the broken section of wall. He started to panic. He wound his legs tighter round the rope and gripped the rope in his hands. A sharp sudden pain struck him as the rope cut deep into his fingers. He could bare it no longer. Five fingers gripped the rope, then four, three, two and finally one. Jack stared at his wee finger willing it to hold on but he couldn't. He let go and began to fall.

Instantly he threw out his other hand and caught the rope ignoring the searing pain. He bit his lower lip desperate to let go but he knew that would be the end of him. He looked down at his feet dangling beneath him and froze

"Don't look down Jack. Lift those feet and wrap them back round the rope. It's your only hope."

Jack's stomach muscles strained as he tried to lift his legs higher into the air but it was useless, he couldn't do it."

Cobs shouted out to him, "Do it for your father."

On hearing the mention of his father, a renewed strength surged through Jack and he flung his leg over the rope. He continued, sweat dripping down onto the granite rocks below, one leg slowly crossing the other, each hand passing over the other until finally he reached the other side and let go. He fell in a heap at Cobs' feet.

"Well done young man!" beamed Cobs.

Jack's face grew red and a strange heat warmed him from the inside. He had never been called a young man before and he liked the sound of it.

"Not far now."

They travelled on along the wall and from their great height, they saw beyond the valley, out to the coastal plains under a silver moon, where golden lights bobbed on the ocean. But inside the wall's boundaries, the night held a different view as though a sinister veil had draped itself over the landscape. Jack could see dark shadows creep over the hillside and burning red eyes blink from within deep crevices. The muffled sounds of the nightfall creatures travelled through the orb and although the sounds were hushed, they still made the hairs on Jack's neck stand on end. He was grateful for the Orb's protection and to the night's darkness for hiding his fear from Cobs.

The wall rose to a peak and soon after they came upon a shallow trench, big enough for them to lie in. Moss and lichen lined its interior making it soft and they hopped down into it. Cobs took his fishing rod from his backpack and extended it.

"Take off your cloak Jack."

Jack removed the spike of hawthorn and took off the silver brooch. He untied the cloak and handed it to Cobs, who shook it, just as though he were placing a fresh sheet on a bed. He draped the cloak over the fishing rod, using it as a tent pole and then tucked the edges into the spaces in the rocks above their heads. They had an instant roof and the warmth of their breath soon made the space beneath cosy.

"We'll be alright in here 'til first light, then we'll head on and be at the peak of Slieve Donard before midday. Now get your head down, you'll need your strength."

"But what about the Shimnavore, Cobs?"

"Get some sleep Jack. I'll worry enough for the both of us."

Chapter 19
Hopscotch

Jack awoke the next morning with a crick in his neck and a spine that felt as though a nighttime army had trampled over it. He stood up and tried to stretch.

"Aaahh…" Jack flinched.

"Aaahh yourself Jack," said Cobs, thinking Jack was enjoying his stretch. "And good morning to ya. I slept like a baby on a mattress. How about you?"

"Baby on a mattress! I feel as though I *was* that blinkin' mattress…."

"Ah you poor wee thing, you weren't built for the hills, that's for sure. Now sit yourself down here."

Jack sat and Cobs pressed his knee into the small of Jack's back. He placed his hands on Jack's shoulders and pulled hard. Jack could hear bones click in places he didn't know he had bones and he could feel muscles stretch in places he didn't know he had muscles.

"Ahhhhh, stop it! You're gonna break my back!"
"There you go. Now stand up."
"After that, I'll be lucky if I can crawl…"
Jack stood up and to his surprise, but more to his delight, his pain had gone.

After their meal of leftover fruit, they climbed out of their bolthole and stood up on the wall. A fresh breeze came off Binnian Mountain and Jack stood breathing in its sweet air, surveying everything around him. Out on the sea where the lights had shone brightly the night before he could make out great swaying masses.

"They're Scadan Jack. They look like huge water creatures, but they're just enormous schools of fish. At night, they reflect the moonlight turning the water golden but in the daylight, they turn the sun's golden rays silver. They're said to guide lost souls home. Let's head on."

The wall skirted along the side of the mountain and began to rise towards another.

"That's Chimney Rock Mountain, Jack, but we're headed to that mountain."

Cobs pointed a stubby index finger into the distance.

"There is Slieve Donard, the king of all the mountains. On the very edge of the Kingdom of Mourne Jack. Not far now."

On seeing Donard Mountain Cobs had a new lease of life and he raced on ahead but Jack stood fixed to the spot staring at the peaks of Chimney Rock Mountain. His eyes strained in the bright sunlight forcing him to lower his head and in that brief moment, he heard a bird call. It was so full of sadness it filled Jack with a great sorrow. He spun around quickly to see what had made the sound but it was too late, it had gone. No - hold on, there it was again, the same sound, only this time it was muffled.

Jack looked beyond the wall, into the Inner Realm, and there he could see the beating wings of a bird in flight.

As it rode the thermal currents, dipping and swaying, flitting back and forth it sang out. Jack caught the glimpse of a snow-white crest amidst the flurry of black feathers. He knew instantly it was the Rare Ring Ouzel but it flew off and the sweet song faded with it. Suddenly another sound filled the air, a familiar tune, a tune he had heard his father whistle many a time and it was coming from up on Chimney Rock Mountain. He no longer cared for the Drewron's prophecy; he could hear the tune his father whistled every day of his life. He scaled down the great wall and sprinted up the mountainside. With every footfall, the sound intensified and Jack hoped beyond all hope that he would find his father waiting for him.

Cobs continued along the wall taking in the panoramic views and humming his own tune not noticing his companion had gone. He knew he was near the end of his journey, for Donard Mountain was the place the Rare Ring Ousel bird lived and it lay just up ahead and nothing could stop him from reaching it.

Jack came to a stop and in front of him near a cliff edge stood a young girl in a red dress. She was still whistling 'Fiddlers Green' and staring straight at him. Although he was bitterly disappointed at it not being his father he quickly realised he was being stupid forever thinking that it could have been. Instead, he approached the young girl and spoke to her.

"Hello there. Where did you come from?"

His surprise to see another human made his voice rise to a shrill squeak and he blushed. He joined her on the outcrop of rock, trying hard not to look down; instead fixing his attention on the young girl. She smiled kindly but didn't reply.

"Where did you come from I said?"

Her watery blue eyes looked towards the ground and Jack's eyes followed hers. He could see roughly drawn squares upon the rocks surface and he laughed when he realised what they were.

"Hopscotch! You're playing hopscotch," laughed Jack.

She just nodded then opened her hand. A stone as smooth as marble and as black as obsidian sat on her palm but Jack watched in surprise at a thick vein of white quartz that ran through its centre. The quartz sparkled in the sunlight like crushed diamonds and it seemed to be flowing within the stone. She offered up her hand but Jack laughed again. She thrust it towards him this time and Jack reluctantly took the stone from her. It felt warm in his grasp.

The girl jerked her head towards the hopscotch. Jack threw the stone and watched it fall on a square marked with a seven. He looked at the young girl and she jerked her head again in the direction of the stone.

Sure no one can see me, he thought.

He hopped and scotched to the square then reached down and picked up the stone. He held it in his hand again, only this time the stone seemed hotter than before. He was about to throw it again when the ground beneath began to rumble and judder. He shook from side to side as each square began to split and tear away from the next one. The numbered hopscotch stones drifted off into the sky, before disintegrating and tumbling into the mile of nothing below.

The square Jack stood upon began to fall apart too and he hung, momentarily weightless, his feet wheeling at great speed below him. He shot a desperate glance back to the girl, but she faded away like a ghostly apparition.

He began to fall and his vision blurred as the cliff face whizzed by, until something struck him.

Everything went black.

Chapter 20
Beyond the Wall

"Wake up! Wake up!"

Jack could see something hazy coming towards him again only this time he caught it as it approached. He held Cobs' hand tightly in his grip.

"Don't hit me again, please."

"You're alright, you're alright!" Cobs hopped about madly. "I only slapped you to make you come round. I'm sorry"

"What happened anyway?"

"It's all my fault Jack. I got so caught up seeing Slieve Donard that I rushed on ahead but I got this really bad feeling and that's when I realised you weren't there. I ran back down the wall but before I could get to you, the cliff you were standing on began to crumble and I saw you fall. You were tumbling towards the wall, straight into the Orb and I thought you were dead for sure."

Jack, still quite groggy, interrupted, "I saw the Rare Ring Ouzel you know and a girl in a red dress."

Cobs looked confused. "You what?"

"I said I saw the rare Ring Ousel, here in the InBetween, but when I saw it again it was in the Inner Realm, beyond the wall. Then I played hop….I mean I got distracted, anyway never mind that bit… there was a girl…. a girl in a faded red dress. She handed me a strange stone and…"

Cobs interrupted, "A strange stone you say! Tell me what it looked like?"

Jack opened his hand and the vein of quartz glistened brightly inside the obsidian black stone.

Cobs face flushed and his eyes widened. He looked all around him, as if suspicious of prying eyes. "Don't let that stone out of your possession. You must protect it with your life do you hear me and more importantly, don't ever let anyone else see it."

"But it's just a stone," said Jack sarcastically.

"You've no idea what it is Jack!" came Cobs' angry retort. "Now hide it quickly and keep it hidden." Cobs took a few deep breaths to calm himself. "There's something I must tell you now Jack and I only hope you can forgive me for not telling the whole truth sooner."

Jack sat upright, hanging on Cobs' every word.

"Do you remember the black pot I showed you in my father's study?" said Cobs.

"Yeah, what about it?"

"Well it was nearly my three hundred and thirty sixth or seventh birthday and I was playing in my father's study. I wasn't watching where I was going and I accidentally fell upon the side of the bureau. To my utter surprise, the side panel popped open and I found a hidden compartment."

Jack's eyes grew larger in anticipation.

"You can only imagine Jack how curious I was to see what was inside. I know I shouldn't have but I couldn't resist. I mean what Clurichaun could? I looked and I found more than just the black pot that I showed you. There was a leather bound book too with a strange crest on it. It wasn't our family crest, Oh no, not a tree in a tree. This one had a crest of three fish swimming in a circle and when I say swimming, I mean it. The fish were swimming over each other, actually moving under the book's leather cover. I'd never seen anything like that kind of magic before and I couldn't help myself. Even though I knew I shouldn't, I looked inside."

"And what was in it?"

"Pages and pages of writing but not written by my father. There were strange diagrams of places and things I'd never seen before. It was impossible to understand any of it. I haven't the time now to explain but the book spoke of the Mourne Wall and so much more."

"But you said you couldn't understand it."

"Yes I know that, but I also told you that now's not the time explain."

Cobs continued to tell the tale. He told it so vividly that Jack closed his eyes and could picture it in his mind.

"The molten fires of Nemour melted the lands and gave birth to the granite rocks. Cooled by the North winds and the driving rains they lay exposed for eons, until The Elderfolk, who travelled by great ships of stone, first landed in Ireland. But Ireland was ravaged by many evil creatures, spirits and sprites. Farms were destroyed, lands lay barren, families divided. It was to be the end of Ireland. So the Elderfolk spilt and shaped the granite rocks and built a mighty wall that runs to the highest peaks and lowest ravines. And they topped every section of that wall with a bewitching capstone. It holds captive, every evil creature that ever tried to take over these lands."

"What evil creatures?"

"Have you ever heard of Banshees, Changelings, Dullahans and Merrows? They're but to name a few."

"I've heard of some of them from my Nanna Tess. She used to tell me scary stories about them every Halloween. She was born on Halloween you know, way back in 1754."

Cobs seemed to calm down when Jack mentioned his great grandmother again.

"Halloween 1754. That was a blue moon birth, Jack, a very special one. Beginning of the year to many."

"Is it? How'd you know that?"

"Because it's the same as mine and on a blue moon as well."

"Halloween and on a blue moon! What year?"

"It would have been…" Cobs concentrated. "The year 1411."

"That's amazing."

"How about you Jack? Were you born on a blue moon?"

"Don't think so. I was born on June 21st."

"What year?"

"1836. I don't think that there was a blue moon that night. I'm sure Nanna would have told me. She did mention someone's birthday like hers once, but she stopped talking about it before she even started. She does that a lot. I used to think she just forgot what she was talking about half way through her sentence, but now I wonder. Sorry Cobs, I didn't mean to interrupt you, you were talking about the wall."

"Ah yes the wall. As I've said, it was built by the Elderfolk. They built it in a perfect circle to hold all the evil creatures of Ireland."

"But Cobs the wall isn't a perfect circle." Jack interrupted again.

"It was a perfect circle up until the Holocene."

"You mentioned that before but you said you didn't know anything more than that."

"I lied Jack."

Jack was shocked. He had thought Cobs incapable of such a thing.

"I should have told you the truth earlier. The Holocene was a war. A war no one thought would ever be waged. After all, every evil creature had been caught inside the wall, trapped within the Silver Orb. But this war was between the Shimnavore, who were the Ancient's war-dogs. They had risen up after the wall was finished and they grew in strength so fast that the Elderfolk feared they would soon break free of the True Kingdom and cross into the Outer Realm. They knew that if the Shimnavore reached there it would be the end of everything. So the Elderfolk used a vast amount of energy and opened their unbreakable wall. It nearly ended everything. The devastation can still be seen to this day. They made a wall that was never meant to be breached you see and in breaking it the very mountains shifted and the wall was stretched out of shape. The Silver Orb became warped."

"Warped?"

"Yes, the Orb was originally a perfect sphere enclosing the circular wall but when the wall was breached the Orb became twisted and deformed like a warped bubble. Once all the Shimnavore were captured inside the Orb, it became impenetrable again. But you Jack…"

"Yes, what about me."

"When I said I waited for you to be bounced off the Orb and killed."

"Yes."

"Well you found its secret instead Jack."

"I did?" said Jack confused.

"Yes. You found the secret of the Silver Orb."

"Can you let me in on it?"

"You see, you didn't exactly bounce off the Orb Jack. You followed the Rare Ring Ouzel just like the Drewron's prophecy."

"Call me stupid but I still don't understand what you're talking about."

"We're on the other side of the wall Jack. You fell through the Orb. You found out that there is a hole in it, a way in, and a way out. That is the secret of the Silver Orb."

Jack looked up at the height of the Mourne Wall.

"You mean we're in the Inner Realm?"

"Yes."

"But how do we get out again?"

"Simple Jack. Look out of the corner of your eye."

Jack made out a thin piece of rope attached to a capstone on the wall. It went upwards and seemed to hang in mid air before falling back to the ground. Where it hung from was the hole in the Orb.

"I watched you fall right through the Orb and I was about to jump into the Inner Realm after you but just before I did I realised there would be no way back out. That's when I knew the Drewron's rope would come in useful."

"Hey, do you think the hole in the Orb is how the Shimnavore's getting out to steal the dandelion clocks?"

"Yes Jack, it has to be. The Shimnavore must know the secret too. We're now the only three who do and that puts us in grave danger. If that creature knew we had seen what it was up to there is no way it would leave us alive."

Jack gulped hard.

Cobs could hear a noise coming from inside his backpack, a bit like a pencil scratching on paper. It grew louder. He pulled out the map, quickly unfurled it, and laid it on the ground. Intricate details of the area inside of the wall were being filled in before his very eyes. He could see winding paths rolling down the mountains and two great lakes, long and thin, running through the centre. One of the lakes had the word 'Happy' crossed out and replaced with the word 'Silent'.

"Look Jack there, near the far corner of that lake."

Jack read the word aloud.

"Bellmouth."

"Yes, from the Drewron's prophecy. Remember? That's where we're headed Jack. But listen good, no one has stepped into the Inner Realm since the Shimnavore and don't forget the evil creatures that were cast here long before them. You saw for yourself how the night changes this place, so we've until sunset before we have to find a place to hide. We don't want to be caught in the open when the creatures surface to crawl these hills."

"Well come on then," said Jack.

They descended the map's newly labelled Rocky Mountain, with the light constantly shifting on the distant hills with each passing cloud. Jack found it hard to believe that such a place of beauty could harbour the night terrors he had witnessed the previous evening. As they walked, Cobs kept checking the map for new names and details of the Inner Realm. He didn't like the sound of the Devil's Coachroad and wondered about the inhabitants mentioned in the Castles beyond it.

Their footing was unsure on the uneven rocks and Jack noticed that Cobs didn't have the confidence of four hundred and thirty seven years walking his familiar pathways.

"We'll head over there Jack, towards that great wall holding back the lake at the bottom of the valley. The map calls it Ben Crom, and then we'll travel into the Valley of Silence towards the Bellmouth."

They followed the natural contours of the mountain but after about a mile Cobs came to an abrupt stop. His pointed ears pricked up further through the holes in his hat, his neck sprang backwards, his nostrils flared and his nose twitched, and great tears began to stream from his eyes.

"Jack, help me!" he screamed before collapsing on the ground.

"Cobs! What's the matter?"

Jack loosened Cobs' collar and placed his ear close to his mouth. He was still breathing. Jack shook him violently, shouting his name repeatedly.

"Get up Cobs, get up!"
There was no response.
The Spirit of Hartshorn. Thought Jack. *The gift from the Staghorn back in Pierce's castle.*

He reached into his waistcoat pocket and removed the small cloth bundle of herbs then placed them under Cobs' nose and squeezed the small package tightly. After a few seconds – that seemed to Jack like days - Cobs began to cough and splutter.

"There's so many of them, too many…" said Cobs as he grabbed his nose and pinched it tightly, "Can't you smell them Jack?"

Jack smiled, glad to have his friend back. "Too many what Cobs? I can't smell a thing."

"Just get me my map."

Jack reached into the backpack, retrieved the map, and rolled it out on the ground.

"There Jack. I must get up there."

Jack looked at the map and back to Cobs. "It's a cave!"

"Well I need to get inside it and take back what is rightfully mine but I can't go any closer. I don't know what would happen to me. What am I to do?"

Jack looked at Cobs who was lying on the ground, shivering and weak.

"I don't know what you need in that cave but I'll go and get it for you," said Jack, knowing that whatever was inside the cave was of great importance to Cobs and that was good enough for him. "But what am I looking for?

Cobs answered in a faint whisper, "You'll know when you see it."

Jack removed his cloak and laid it over Cobs then he began the steep climb over the loose gravel and rugged boulders. His ankles twisted and strained on the rough ground and as he climbed higher, he could see deep horizontal lines running across the mountain's face and then he spied the narrow opening to the cave. He stood outside, afraid to enter. Whatever was inside had caused Cobs to faint. Why hadn't it affected him? He had to help his friend. He had no choice.

He breathed in and squeezed through the tiny opening. Darkness immediately engulfed him, but he didn't panic, instead he felt for his leather pouch on his belt and loosened the cord around its small wooden button. He took out the candle Neiron had given him then licked his thumb and index finger before squeezing on the candle's wick. It began to glow, and then spontaneously burst into flame lighting up the cave's narrow walls with a strange yet familiar golden hue. He smiled at the thought of how the candle lit.

Jack edged his way forward, forced to stoop by the cave's low ceiling. Beneath his boots were pools of slime-green water filled with the bones of different creatures, none of which Jack had ever seen before. He tried to ignore the sound of them crunching and shattering underfoot as he stepped further into the cave. As he moved forward, he came to a wall and could go no further but just above his head, he could make out a ledge. He had to reach up and tilt the candle onto a high ledge to drip some hot wax then he sat the candle into it.

Jack hoisted himself up and found himself at the mouth of another chamber. It was narrower then the one he had just come through and thoughts of being stuck between the walls started to fill his head.

A strange overpowering smell filled the air and Jack's eyes began to sting but he gulped hard and held his breath. He had no choice but to travel on. He lifted his candle and crawled onward on all fours to the entrance of a third chamber.

What he found inside made him stop dead in his tracks.

Chapter 21
Inside the Cave

Cobs knew he'd sent a boy to do the job of a Clurichaun and the pangs of guilt made him feel worse than he already did. He had to go and help Jack. As he struggled to his feet, something on the ground caught his eye. It was the map. He picked it up and there on the place marked 'Byshee Cave' he could see a tiny blue light. For some strange reason the map seemed to know Jack's whereabouts even without the compass sitting on it.

Cobs headed towards the cave but with every step, the strange smell grew stronger and he grew even dizzier. He squeezed on Jack's bag of herbs and inhaled repeatedly until his head began to pound. Although his strength was almost spent he forced himself to carry on but after another few steps, he had to stop. His left arm felt heavy and a strange deadening sensation ran through it. He bit on his fingertips but they felt numb as if they were inside a leather glove, then his stomach began to ache and spasm in rhythm with the tremendous thumping inside his head. He fell to his knees too weak to go any further.

Jack held up his candle and its light reflected and scattered in all directions. He could see that the walls were made of white crystals.

No hold on, he thought, *they aren't crystals.*

But what he saw next made him forget about the walls. He took a quick step backwards for in front of him, in the centre of the cave, slept a giant beast, its hulking ribcage rising and falling with every snarled intake of breath. Jack looked to the end of its sinewy limbs where claws, sharper than his father's cut-throat razor, lay open. The creature grunted and began to stir, shifting on the bare floor until the back of its head faced Jack. Much to his relief the beast's eyes were firmly shut. It yawned widely, bearing fangs that jutted through red raw gums right into a thick upper lip. A foul stink escaped its mouth and Jack choked. Afraid he would waken the beast and knowing he couldn't defend himself if he did, he quickly fled the cave.

Sunlight welcomed Jack's face and he sighed deeply, grateful for his freedom but it was short-lived for there half way down the mountainside he spied Cobs. Without a moment's hesitation he rushed down over the loose rocks until he was by his side. Cobs looked up at him, and then hung his head.

"I'm so sorry. I should never have let you go on your own," said Cobs, his voice low and husky.

"But I knew you couldn't help it. You look worse than when I left you."

"I feel worse Jack. I think if I had tried to get any further you'd have found me dead."

"Let's get away from here. I promise you'll feel better once we do."

Jack left his cloak around Cobs' shoulders and he helped him off the mountainside, with every step further away from the cave he could see Cobs' rosy colour return to his cheeks.

"Tell me about the cave Jack. What did you find there?"

"It stank," said Jack, wrinkling his nose. "It was full of strange skeletons and half-eaten things."

"All well and good, but tell me about the cave itself, Jack."

"There were three chambers in it and in the last one I found out that it wasn't all the dead creatures making the smell," said Jack.

"What was it?"

"It was the Shimnavore."

"The Shimnavore!" cried Cobs.

"Yes. It was lying on the ground asleep so I got a good look inside the third chamber before I ran for it. At first I thought the walls were made of crystal just like in the cave under Cloc Mor but they weren't crystals Cobs, they were....."

"...they were dandelion clocks!" interrupted Cobs.
"Yes, but how'd you know?"
"I could smell them. That's what overpowered me. But they're not just dandelion clocks Jack. They're stolen dandelion clocks. They are the stolen wishes of countless children. A hundred years worth of broken promises..."

"The whole of the third chamber was lined with them Cobs, all except for a small part no bigger than my thumb," said Jack.

"The Shimnavore has been lining that cave with the clocks of the dandelions for nearly a century and if it finishes what it intends to do... it would be catastrophic for everyone!"

Jack could see the terror on Cobs' face. It reminded him of the look his mother had when she told him his father had been lost at sea.

Cobs checked his pocket watch and pressed the winder twice to see the compass, and then he flicked it back to the clock face and repeated his actions several times.

"I haven't much time. I haven't much time," he repeated. "I've got to get to the Bellmouth as quick as I can. It's all part of the Drewron's prophecy… it's my only choice….yes my only choice." Cobs paused for a moment; he seemed to be talking to himself for not once did he make eye contact with Jack. Then he began to mutter again.

"That's it. Yes that's definitely it." He stared straight up at the boy and with a voice full of authority he commanded, "Go back to the wall and climb out the way you fell in. You have come far enough. Now you must go home."

Jack couldn't believe his ears. He hadn't come this far only to be shooed away like a stray pup. He snarled at Cobs, "No way! My wish is just waiting to happen….I will get my father back …and not you or nobody is gonna stop me."

For a moment, Jack wanted to hit Cobs but when he saw the look of fear on the tiny creature's face he realised he was only trying to protect him.

"I'm coming whether you like it or not!"

Chapter 22
Silence and Bellmouth

Jack never spoke a word to Cobs as they crossed the open heathland. He was still angry at being told to leave and he wanted Cobs to know it. After a short while, they came across old quarry tracks that led to a small lake. Cobs stopped to take a drink but Jack raced onward, sweat pooling behind his earlobes and dripping from his brow. Small midges had gathered over his head and when he looked back to see where Cobs was, he was forced to look through a buzzing swarm of tiny black dots. No matter how many times he tried to swat them, they just gathered in greater numbers.

"They seem to like you Jack," shouted Cobs.

"That's not even funny Cobs, now come on." Jack marched off.

"No Jack, we have to pace ourselves. If you keep going on like this you'll wear yourself out."

Although he didn't want to admit it, Jack knew Cobs was right. He wanted to get to the Bellmouth as quickly as possible, but arriving there half-dead would be of no use to anyone, so he decided to stop and rest too.

"I'm sorry for ordering you to go home Jack."

"I know and I'm sorry for snapping at you as well."

"We're a right pair aren't we? Anyway, Jack, I've been looking at the map again. It is truly 'amazing', as you keep saying when you see something new that I just take for granted. I know names of places that I've only ever seen from outside the wall. I must show you something truly wonderful. Come on, you should've got your breath back by now."

They set off once again, walking a short distance, travelling higher along the track until they came to a spot with a bird's eye view over a long valley. Cobs held the map in front of him. "It's called the Silent Valley. The word Happy is written just above it but it has been scored out."

At the bottom of the valley lay two long but narrow lakes and a vast dam that by Jack's reckoning was nearly half a mile high.

"Who on earth could have built that?" asked Jack. His eyes were as wide as they were when he first saw the Curraghard Tree.

"Only the Elderfolk; those blocks that make it up must weigh twenty of me and the dam has to be ten times the height o' the Mourne Wall. But we can't stay to admire their work; we have to go into the Valley of Silence."

They crossed through the saddle of the mountains and began their descent.

"Hey that's weird Cobs. Look at that tree down there. It's the only one in the whole valley."

"Hey, you're right. We'll head towards it."

The bare menacing slopes of the mountain on the other side of the lake towered over them and began to fill their view as they zigzagged down through the marshy hills until they arrived at the lone tree. Its branches hung heavy, touching the ground marking a midway point between the two great lakes.

As they passed the tree, Jack heard a humming noise, like a swarm of angry bees. After another step, the sound changed to a high-pitched ringing followed quickly by hissing. Finally, a screech so shrill filled the air, forcing him to stuff his fingers in his ears. Then in an instant, the sounds were gone. Jack was grateful for the silence but it didn't last long for he soon realised he couldn't hear a thing. He had been struck deaf. He turned to Cobs for help but he could see that he had his fingers stuffed into his long pointed ears.

Jack dashed back towards the lone tree and when he reached it, his hearing returned. He beckoned Cobs who followed straight away.

"That noise was unbelievable; when it finally stopped I couldn't hear a thing. What about you Jack?"

"Me neither," replied Jack flicking his ears with his fingertips, glad to have his hearing back.

"It must be why they call it the Silent Valley. If we're to pass through it we'll just have to do without our hearing."

They edged past the lone tree again. This time the terrible noises weren't as painful and when the last screams stopped they were both deaf again.

Cobs suddenly wanted to tell Jack something that he felt was important but his hand gestures and twisted faces didn't make him any clearer.

"Cobs! I haven't a clue what you're trying to say," shouted Jack.

Jack's voice lifted into the air and grew louder as it echoed off the surrounding hills but being deaf, neither Cobs nor Jack could hear it. They only realised something was wrong when the first rocks began to fall. Jack's voice had set off an avalanche. Rock after rock fell from the sky.

They couldn't tell where the next rock would land, for they were too busy trying to dodge the previous one. Cobs tugged frantically on Jack's cloak and pointed.

"There. Over there," he mouthed.

Jack looked in the direction Cobs was pointing.

The lake. The rocks hadn't reached that far yet. Jack rushed towards it and when he reached the water's edge, he spun around to see where Cobs was. A rock glanced off Cobs' shoulder bringing him to his knees. Jack could do nothing but stand hopeless. From the anguished look on Cobs' face, he knew he was screaming. Jack took a sharp intake of breath and ignored the peril he was about to put himself into. He sprinted towards Cobs, dodging the falling rocks. A sideward step here and a quick jump to the left, then right and a final dart and he was at Cobs' side. He grabbed Cobs' arm and lifted him high into the air then flung him over his shoulder.

With Cobs now secure, he made another dash for the lakeside. The ground cracked open with every footfall but Jack battled on. He wasn't about to let his quest end like this. He reached the waterside, dropped Cobs in a heap, and fell to his knees fighting for breath.

But the rocks kept falling, they didn't let up no matter how exhausted Jack felt.

Suddenly a sharp pain stabbed into Jack's thigh. He thought he'd been struck too. He looked down half-expecting to see blood, but there was none. The pain grew worse and now he could smell his flesh burning. He delved inside his trouser pocket and pulled out the object that was searing into his skin. It was his toy boat and it was roasting hot. Even though it hurt to hold it, he didn't want to let it go. His father had made it for him. Jack tossed it from one hand to the other but it didn't help. He could hold it no longer. The boat fell from his hands and landed on the lake.

Cobs felt a surge of heat and he turned in the direction of the lake. He signalled to Jack, trying to ask him what had just happened but all Jack could do was point to his burnt leg then point back to the boat. Cobs shot a glance at the water and grinned.

"That's it," Cobs mouthed, he put his open hands to the sides of his face and wriggled his fingers trying to mime something.

"What the heck are you doing?" Jack mouthed.

Cobs, who still couldn't hear a thing, took finger and thumb, and made a plucking gesture. Jack just threw his hands up in exasperation. He hadn't a clue what his friend was trying to tell him.

The rocks continued their deadly assault but Cobs still couldn't make himself understood. He gave up trying and dived on Jack tearing at the leather pouch on his belt then he grabbed the flower from inside and thrust it into Jack's face.

It was the shrinking violet that Veronica had given Jack on the night of the ball in Pierce's castle. Cobs put his finger and thumb together then made the plucking action again. Jack nodded, finally understanding him.

They each took hold of the flower and ripped off a petal.

First, the muscles on the back of Jack's hand started to tic and spasm, followed quickly by his forearm that twitched and shook. Next, his elbow jerked backwards straight into his own ribcage. Before he could fully register what was happening the twitch became a sudden cramp and a horrific pain swept across his body. His heart raced, his palms dripped sweat, and his eyes blurred so much he could hardly see. He willed his body to stop shaking but the more he tried the more it convulsed. His eyes blinked rapidly and his head twisted forcibly to the right. It felt as though he were slipping down through his own body, inside his own skin.

The mountains seemed to stretch and grow around him and the far side of the lake now seemed miles away. The lake itself had become a vast ocean. The heathers and grasses were now as big as forests.

Jack tried to concentrate on a single object to get his bearings and when he did, he realised.

Everything hadn't grown.

It was he who had shrunk. And so had Cobs.

Jack and Cobs still couldn't hear one another so trying to explain the shock of what just happened would have to wait.

Jack looked to where he had dropped his boat desperately hoping it hadn't sunk. To his relief it hadn't. The boat was sitting proudly on the water and given their newfound size; it could easily take both of them.

The symbol on the bow glowed like a beacon and Cobs stood staring at it, mesmerised.

The rocks still fell from the sky only now they were as big as houses and if either of them were hit, they would be squashed as easy as a tiger beetle.

Jack grabbed Cobs and mouthed the word, "JUMP."

They held hands and leapt towards the boat, their free arms and legs thrashing about as they hurtled through the air. The moment they hit the wooden boards with a crash their hearing returned.

"Whoa Jack! Veronica could have warned us. I've never felt anything like that in my entire life."

"And I for one don't ever want to again. What size do you think we are now, anyway?"

"No bigger than her finger, she said if I remember rightly. About the size of an inchworm. I think that's why the lake looks like the size of an ocean now."

Enormous granite boulders dive-bombed into the lake sending crushing waves against their boat, tossing it about on the angry water. Cobs was petrified, but as Jack looked at the rudder of the boat he felt calm and safe, for sitting at the helm was the carving of a fisherman; perfect in every detail, right down to the basket weave stitch on its Aran jumper. Jack clawed his way towards the statue as the howling seas crashed around him. He sat next to it, placing his hand into his. He traced the carved lines along its palm and felt a small bump, just like a wee rope burn.

Jack took a deep breath and leaned over the side of the boat. A ripple-wrinkled face with foam-greyed hair looked back at him, the same face that was at the pier the morning he waited for his father. This time the reflection didn't fill him with dread, instead it was almost welcome as though it were trying to help him. He closed his eyes half-aware of what he was doing, and placed his open hand on the water. For an instant, the water froze around his palm then the sounds of a thousand whispers pressed against the surface, crying for release.

The bow of the boat rose up at a sharp angle and its stern dropped heavily. Water gushed onto the deck nearly swamping the boat. Cobs frantically scooped handfuls back over the side, but it was hopeless.

"We're going to sink!"

Jack didn't reply, instead he reached into the waters again. This time the whispers became roars as they broke free of their prison. Cobs covered his ears as a storm began to rage around them and the screaming voices from the lake merged with the howling of the winds.

All the while Jack sat perfectly still, his eyes fixed, staring into the face of the carved fisherman.

The waves capped with ghost-white foam leapt around the hull lifting it high into the air and soon the boat was riding on the back of a monstrous wave. The broken mast on the deck crashed towards them, Cobs clung to the boat's side waiting for its impact, but Jack remained motionless, still staring into the eyes of the carving at the rudder. They were at the mercy of the lake, whose endless expanse surged all around them. Cobs edged his way towards Jack and pulled hard on his boot but the lad didn't budge so he opened his mouth wide and bit Jack hard on the ankle, trying to get a response but still there was none…

The boat rode higher on the back of the stampeding wave, past the mountains on the distant shores. Cobs could see a massive granite wall looming up ahead. They were making a direct line towards it.

"Jack! Jack! For goodness sake, snap out of it."

He sank his teeth into Jack's ankle again and this time Jack flinched.

"Oi! What do you think you're doing?"

"Look ahead. That wall, we're gonna hit it!"

Jack closed his eyes and squeezed the thumb of the carved wooden hand. Immediately, the boat shifted course.

"It's working Jack, whatever you're doing, it's working."

When Cobs looked out over the bow, Jack saw his face turn white.

"Now look where we headed!"

It was a powerful whirlpool at the edge of the lake and it was sucking the boat into its hungry churning waters. No matter how hard Jack pressed on the carved hand, the boat didn't change course. In fact, when they reached the lake's outer rim the boat picked up great speed. Jack looked over the side and to his shock he saw they were travelling on a whirlpool of flowing earth and stone.

"We're in the Bellmouth!" shouted Cobs, "and it's taking us down."

Jack looked all about him to see if there was anything that could help. The fisherman at the helm was lifeless, the rudder wouldn't budge but there on his friend's back was the answer. He grabbed hold of Cobs' backpack and pulled out the fishing rod just as the boat scraped over the lip of the Bellmouth. He cast the fishing line and waited for it to catch on something but it didn't and the horizon was quickly devoured as they began their rapid descent.

Jack reeled in the fishing line as fast as he could trying to ignore the maelstrom about him. He looked up and saw the circle of daylight getting smaller as they were submerging into the lake. He cast off for a second time. The line flew upwards towards the edge of the Bellmouth but again it didn't catch and began to fall again. It scraped between the crevice of two large rocks and somehow, beyond hope, the hook caught.

Jack didn't waste a second, he quickly fastened the other end of the line to the bow and shouted to Cobs to hold onto something and brace himself. The boat gave a sudden jolt as the fishing line strained to near breaking point. The boat stopped falling. It hung, vertical, against the Bellmouth wall. Jack and Cobs clung on to the half-broken mast and Jack watched in horror as the other half fell into the void below.

"We've stopped Jack. You did it."

No sooner had the words left Cobs' mouth when the high waters of the lake above broke violently over the edge of the Bellmouth and hit the boat. The fishing line couldn't hold any more weight and it snapped.

The boat plummeted into the stony vortex.

Chapter 23
Beneath the Lake

Jack and Cobs held on tight to the mast as they spiralled widdershins down into the depths of the lake. They were so far below the surface that all they could see were the muddy water-walls of the hole. Jack closed his eyes, praying for some miracle. Drowning was his worst nightmare. The boat was within an inch of the lake's floor when the ground split open and swallowed it whole.

They continued to fall for some time but through thin air, for now they were beneath the lake. Finally, the boat crashed down onto granite cobbles, skidded across a long darkened tunnel and smashed against a wall of carved rock, coming to rest in a crevice no bigger than a mouse hole.

"We've made it Jack, we've made it," shouted Cobs.

Jack's recent spurt of bravery had gone as quickly as it had come and the young boy began to panic.

"I know, I know, but where on earth have we made it to?"

"Aren't you just glad to be alive Jack? That hole we just fell through could have killed the both of us."

As Jack sat on the boat trying to get his bearings, the shadows on the opposite wall distracted him. Were they moving? Surely it was just a trick of the light? He squeezed the palm of the wooden fisherman pretending not to notice, convincing himself he had to be wrong. But this time the shadows twisted then writhed along the length of the corridor. He tried even harder to ignore them but the more he tried the more frightened he felt. He imagined their dark invisible fingers running over him and the thought chilled his bones.

"Cobs, I don't like this place. Those shadows over there on the walls, they have no one to be shadows for."

"I know Jack, I've noticed them too. They're not really shadows, that's why."

"Then what are they?"

"They're Banshees. They just move amongst the shadows but don't worry we're far too small for even them to notice us…..I hope."

"What!"

"Well I'm no expert. I've only ever read about them. They were said to take on many a form but there's worse things than just seeing them. To hear the Banshee's wail means that death isn't far behind."

Jack had a sudden image of the shadows back at home just before he found himself in the forest. He tried his best to remember if he heard them wail but his macabre thoughts were interrupted by the sound of galloping hooves that got louder as they approached and echoed off the walls scaring the shadows away. Jack and Cobs stayed where they were and watched as a black stallion and a filthy goat-like creature raced past.

"They're Pookah Jack, goblin-folk. They wreaked havoc on many a farmer in your Realm."

"They look like they're running scared from something."

"Or someone."

Over the next ten minutes the stone corridor saw many a strange foot trample through it and Cobs named each creature as it passed.

"They're Merrows Jack," said Cobs pointing to half a dozen fish-like creatures that rushed past holding on tightly to red-feathered caps in their webbed fingers. "They're not usually land dwellers and neither is this next crowd coming down the corridor."

A horde of gossamer-winged fairy-like creatures flew past.

"They look harmless enough," said Jack.

"Don't be fooled. They aren't like the fairies you met. These are Watershee Jack, deadly water spirits and they brought down many an innocent in the marshy grounds in the bogs of Allen."

"Now you can't tell me this next crowd could do any harm. They're children for goodness sake."

A group of about fifteen or twenty scruffy infants paraded past, two by two, holding hands, each with their finger on their lips. Jack was surprised that children this young could even walk.

"They're worse than the Watershee, they're Changelings. They are probably ten times the age of me. Senile fairies, Jack. They'd throw a baby from its cot and take its place."

"But where are they all headed in such a hurry?"

"How should I know? Before now, I didn't even think all these races could exist together within the Orb let alone live under one roof. We have to follow them."

Jack and Cobs took shelter in the real shadows along the edge of the rough stone floor and they scurried as fast as they could, trying to keep up with the creatures but because of their tiny size they soon fell behind. After a few minutes, they reached the end of the corridor but there was no one to be found. They'd lost them.

Instead, a towering set of rusted iron doors stood in front of them, bolted shut from the outside by a carved silver padlock. From behind the door, Jack thought he could hear voices raised in anger.

"Psssst…. Jack…. Look. Over there," whispered Cobs.

They ran along the bottom of the door and stopped below an enormous brass hinge.

"Do you think we'll fit?"

"Course we will, come on."

They crept through a small crevice between the doorframe and the door and found themselves in a great circular chamber.

Chapter 24
Assembly

Jack and Cobs stood dumfounded.

It seemed that every inhabitant from the Inner Realm was there, jostling for space, filling the chamber with their stench, arguing with one another as to who had the right to sit where. Row upon row of granite stone benches descended from dizzying heights like giant steps until they reached the edge of a dark circular pool of water. It was a moat surrounding a raised platform and in it swam the Merrows and Watershee.

Flames erupted from huge torches anchored to the dungeon walls, lighting up the room. Jack stood by the door and breathed in an air thick with anger and fright. Sulphurous red eyes stared down from every angle and that scared him the most.

"This Assembly is in session and I, Chief Dullahan, will hear all gathered. There will be no mention of the Bellmouth. Anyone who does will be dealt with swiftly."

The clanking and clattering of hooves stopped and the raucous shouts of everyone fell to silenced whispers. Jack looked in all directions trying to figure out who had spoken. Then a fright took hold of him for now he could see what had made the noise. It was the stuff of nightmares. On the raised platform, in the centre of the pool, stood a tall figure dressed in black velvet with a black leather cloak resting on its shoulders that hung all the way to its boots. It would have been taller except for one thing and that is what filled Jack with dread most of all. The figure had no head, just an empty space on his neck where a head should have been.

"Silence forsaken ones!" it commanded. The voice seemed to come from nowhere and everywhere at the same time.

"Jack, do you know what this is?" whispered Cobs.
"Yes. It's an Assembly. I heard that bit when I came in?"

"Yes, but do you know what an Assembly is?"
"No." replied Jack."

"It means there must be a form of law here and that headless creature dressed in black is a Dullahan. It is their leader. The Dullahan used to ride on the back of a black steed and thundered through the countryside and wherever it stopped one of your kind died. But the best bit Jack, is that we can listen in. We're so small no one'll notice us."

The Dullahan raised its pale hand and pointed a long grimy finger at a horned creature high up in the chamber.

"Speak."

"I have lost four of my kind in the past three moons and I can't afford to lose any more."

"The Shimnavore likes your kind I know. Finds them sweet," replied the Dullahan.

"It's had ten of us in the End Season." The shout came from a creature Jack now recognised as a Pookah.

"Twelve of us," screamed the Merrow in the water.

"This is not an auction, to see who can outdo the previous bidder. We're all in this together since the Decree of our Forefathers."

The Dullahan's voice shook the room. "We fought for three Ages, from when we were first cast here by the Elderfolk but the Decree put end to that."

At the mention of the word 'Elderfolk', the room erupted in a rush of whispers.

"Silence…"
The room hushed.
"We united against our greatest foe and now only one Shimnavore remains. The rest have gone from our realm, and for that we are grateful, but the one left behind has more than made up for their appetite. It comes as it pleases into our once hidden city and takes who or what ever it wants. We're helpless to stop it," said the Dullahan.

"We should move to a new hiding place," roared the shadow creature in the corner of the circular room.

"We have nowhere left to hide. The Shimnavore can find us anywhere," said the Dullahan

The voice of a child-like creature in the front row shouted out, "This is our never ending Assembly and nothing ever comes from it."

Jack gazed upon its delicate features and watched as they distorted. Its spine grew crooked, the once pale skin turned green and scaly and its left arm shriveled up tucking itself under an armpit. It was a Changeling.

"What would you have us do, Babog? We cannot give up," said the Dullahan.

"I know," replied Babog. "Its voice was not what Jack expected to come from a child. It sounded like an old man. It continued to speak. "But it never seems to go after the Banshees. I have often wondered if they'd made a pact."

"How dare you, Babog," retorted a Banshee, now hovering over the Changeling's head, "we've lost our fair share, we just choose not to mention it in the bidding wars at the start of every Assembly."

The meeting dragged on for some time and as the torches began to fade the creatures rose from their benches and no amount of shouting from the Dullahan could stop them leaving.

"We shall gather at the next Blue Moon."

"That's not 'til next Samhain Jack and not even this year," said Cobs.

The room emptied and Jack and Cobs were left alone with only the Dullahan remaining. It slumped into its throne in the centre of the vast pool of water and let out a wail.

A sudden twitch flew up Jack's left forearm.
"Ouch! Hey Cobs."
"Not now Jack...."
The twitch spread the length of his entire body shaking it so fast that his muscles heated up and felt like they were about to melt.

"Cobs!"
"For goodness sake, Jack, will you be quiet!"

Jack's heartbeat began to slow and his left palm dried up and started to itch. His pupils grew to tiny focused pinpoints. He tried to will his body to move but instead it turned to jelly.

"Don't say I didn't warn you," he muttered.

His eyes blinked slower as his head slumped to the left; any further and he knew it would break. It was as though he was going burst out through his own body. In a matter of seconds, the room grew smaller as he returned to normal size.

Cobs looked up at his now gigantic friend. The effects of the shrinking violet had not worn off him yet and he knew it would be better if he didn't hang around until they did. He spied a space under a bench but as he sprinted towards it, his left foot decided to return to near-normal size. He dragged it behind him and by the time he'd reached the safety of the hidey-hole he had returned to full size.

"What intrusion is this?"
Jack trembled as the voice hit his chest.
"I'll have you flogged for this."
"I'm sorry sir. I didn't mean to upset anyone," said Jack.
"Quiet, thing…. I have never laid eyes on anything so…so… what are you supposed to be anyway?"

"I'm Jack sir…. Jack Turner…. A boy sir."

"A boy sir!" the Dullahan's voice boomed. "Come closer boy."

Jack took a few nervous steps towards the pool but he had no way to cross. He looked over to the Dullahan, who just waved a dismissive hand. Jack was astounded as the stones in the centre platform shook, then one by one; they lifted into the air and stretched out across the moat forming a bridge. It spanned from the Dullahan's boots all the way to Jack. Jack stepped onto the first section and the stones wobbled beneath him but he crossed it bravely and stood in front of the Dullahan.

"Kneel before me boy! First, tell me how you got into this Assembly chamber, let alone into the Inner Realm."

"I'm afraid I don't know," said Jack. He choked on his fear knowing he might only have one chance to state his case.

"Don't know....You, boy, are a liar!"

As the Dullahan roared, it reached down and grabbed Jack by the throat lifting him clean off his feet. He dangled off the ground suspended in the noose-like grip of the Dullahan, choking for air, scared out of his wits. As the blood drained from his head, he knew it was only a matter of seconds before he would lose consciousness. He reached down into his waistcoat pocket and fumbled about but what he was searching for wasn't there. In a flash he realised he'd put it in the other pocket. He moved his hand across his chest slowly, all the while staring in the empty space where the Dullahan's eyes should have been, hoping it wouldn't notice what he was up to. In the other pocket, he found his small leather pouch.

Jack tried not to show his sense of relief as he struggled with the thin drawstring. Finally after a few failed attempts he managed to widen the top of the pouch a fraction.. He swung his arm in a great arc and released the contents.

The Drewron's golden sands scattered into the air and glimmered like dust caught in splintered sunbeams even though the chamber was nearly in darkness. As the sands fell, a family of exquisite voices sang out and Jack knew this was his only chance to get free. In his mind, he could hear himself shout the command for the Dullahan to let him go but as he tried to utter the words through his nearly crushed windpipe, he couldn't manage a croak. But he didn't need to speak for the Dullahan lifted him up and drew him close as though to inspect him. Jack heard him grunt and the next thing he knew he was flying through the air.

Jack landed on the harsh granite floor and squealed like a kicked dog as his shoulder flooded with pain for it had taken the brunt of his fall. But the Dullahan showed no mercy. It just towered over Jack.

"Don't dare try your trickery here boy!" growled the Dullahan, "Those sands don't work on this side of the wall, let alone on someone like me." The Dullahan raised his boot over Jack's head. "Now prepare to meet your maker, you insignificant bug."

Chapter 25

Awakening

Jack lay cowering in a heap, staring up at the Dullahan's boot as it came crashing down towards him. It was the last thing he ever expected to see. But just as his cheek met with the leather sole a voice cried out.

"STOP! "

The pain Jack expected never came; instead, the Dullahan's boot hovered just above him. Cobs didn't waste a moment, he bounded across the bridge as fast as his stubby legs would go. The Dullahan watched as Cobs approached and sensing no danger he put his boot back to the ground and decided to sit on his throne.

Cobs stood in front of Jack, his arms outstretched as if to protect his companion.

"If anyone is looking for their maker it's me," said Cobs. "This young one has risked his life to get this far and who are you to stop him?"

"Who am I…? Who am I…?" The Dullahan shifted on its throne. "Who are you, impudent one?"

"I am Cobs that's who. Son of Poitin." Cobs' face remained stern but he hid his fear well for Jack could see that he was quaking in his boots.

Deafening sounds like the claps of thunder erupted from deep within the Dullahan. Its body shook so hard it had to hold on tight to the arms of the throne. It was the sound of laughter and it lasted for a long time but when it finally stopped, the Dullahan spoke.

"Not for five generations have I smiled, and now you, no higher than the top of my boot have made me laugh. Tell me Clurichaun what gives you such bravery?"

"Knowledge!" Cobs was startled that the Dullahan knew what he was but he did his best to hide that emotion.

"Knowledge of what?" asked the Dullahan

"Of what is to come?" replied Cobs.

"And prey tell, son of Poitin, what do you think is to come?"

On hearing Cobs speak Jack felt a wave of courage wash over him and although he was in a lot of pain, he stood up.

"He knows what I know sir."

"Ah…" said the Dullahan, "Found your voice have we boy… Speak!"

"We know that everything will end soon," said Jack bravely, "and not even the Silver Orb will protect you."

"Impossible," shouted the Dullahan.

"Is it?" said Jack, "I've seen it with my own two eyes."

"You lie… What have you seen?"

"I have seen the Shimnavore's lair," said Jack.

"And what could that possibly have to do with the end of everything?" asked the Dullahan.

"Simple," replied Jack, "The cave the Shimnavore lay in was lined with dandelion clocks."

The Dullahan sat bolt upright on its throne, "Is that all you have to tell me?"

"There is nothing to lose now," said Cobs to Jack. "You may as well tell him everything since you're the one that found it."

"Found what?" shouted the Dullahan growing impatient.

Jack ignored the raised voice and calmly replied. "I have found the secret of the Silver Orb."

"The Silver Orb! The Orb that has held all of us captive for eons. What secret could it possibly hold?"

Jack smiled. "Didn't you think it strange when I said the Shimnvore's lair was covered in dandelion clocks? Think hard Dullahan, dandelions don't grow inside the Orb. The clocks in the Shimnavore's lair are the stolen wishes of thousands of children; children who were given the secret of making a dandelion wish come true just like me."

"Those clocks hold the most powerful magic in all the realms," said Cobs.

"And the only way the Shimnavore could have its claws on them was if it had found a way out of the Orb," shouted Jack.

"Never..." gasped the Dullahan.

"Yes. There is a hole in the Orb. I fell through it and Cobs followed me in. How else do you think we got here?" said Jack.

"Even if a creature could escape the Orb, the Elderfolk's curse made sure it couldn't live outside for long. That curse holds us captive as much as the capstones on the Mourne Wall or even the Orb itself," said the Dullahan.

"Then maybe that's why it's the last of its kind. The rest must have perished collecting the dandelion clocks," said Cobs.

"Unfortunately what you say makes sense…there were so many Shimnavore here a hundred years ago but we never knew where they all went. We were just grateful for their demise."

"There may be only one Shimnavore left but one is enough. There aren't many clocks needed to fill the gap in the cave," said Jack. "I'd say one more visit to the InBetween should do it. When that cave is complete the Shimnavore can make an eternity of evil wishes. It will be the end of everything."

The Dullahan stood up and began pacing. The clacking of its boots echoed off the walls in the dim chamber. "There would have been a time when the inhabitants of this Realm would have been grateful for an end, but not now. They have overcome their differences and forged friendships never thought possible. They no longer even care to be free of the Orb. All they want is to escape the Shimnavore. But what can be done now?"

Jack looked towards the Dullahan. "We were given a prophecy and so far everything has come true, but one thing has yet to be explained. The prophecy told of a bird, the Rare Ring Ousel, the wall, and even the Bellmouth. But it spoke of a place where teardrops fall."

On hearing the words, the Dullahan stopped pacing. "The reason for the Assembly tonight was because of the great wave on the lake. We too have a prophecy. It speaks of a time when a bird flies into our realm and soon after teardrops will fall destroying all in its path. I do not know about the bird but I believe the teardrops are the lake waters that fell. Since this city was built, the lake has never breached the Bellmouth, not until today. This city is destined to perish."

"Then maybe our destinies are one in the same," said Cobs, "we could help each another."

"I swear as I stand on this Assembly Pillar that I will do anything, to stop this city from falling," said the Dullahan.

Jack looked at Cobs and smiled. "Did you just hear what he said Cobs? He said Pillar. This platform in the middle of the moat is the Pillar. It has to be the Pillar from the Drewron's prophecy."

Jack walked to the edge of the pillar and stared into the depths of the water. The reflection of the ripple-wrinkled face with foam-grey hair looked back at him only this time to Jack's amazement it winked. Then a moment later, it mouthed the words 'Follow me.'

Jack desperately wanted to do what it asked but there was no way he could go in after it. Looking into the water was enough to fill him with dread. He remembered what his mother had told him to do when he felt this way. He shut his eyes and imagined the last time he felt safe. Slowly the image came to him. He was sitting high on his father's shoulders laughing for all he was worth. Not only did the image calm him it suddenly gave him a new-fledged hope. All Jack ever wanted was to make his father proud and now he would.

He stepped off the Pillar.

The instant Jack hit the water, his newfound confidence abandoned him and he began to panic. His arms clamoured for something to hold on to, but there was nothing, no hand reached down to rescue him. His legs kicked out, trying to find purchase, but they found none. He was surrounded by darkness, darker than any night he could remember and he couldn't tell up from down or left from right.

Suddenly Jack could hear a voice calling from the distance. It grew louder until he recognised it as the voice he'd heard when he was drowning in Fofanny Dam. It was his brother's voice and comforted him. He no longer felt afraid and he stopped struggling and let himself fall.

When Jack reached the bottom of the moat, a ghostly figure stood waiting for him. It had a contented smile and a face full of warmth. Jack reached out to touch the vision of his brother, Edmund, but it faded quickly and his palm pressed against the base of the Assembly pillar.

The moment his hand touched the bare rock it began to crumble and fall. A scorching white light burst forth and Jack, who had no air left in his lungs, knew he had no choice but to walk into it.

Air rushed into his mouth quickly filling his lungs. He was overjoyed when he found himself in another chamber. He stood on a carpet of snow-white heather that not only covered the floor but lined the granite walls as well. He looked back to where he'd just entered and could see a wall of dark water hovering in mid air, just like in the maze under Cloc Mor stone. As he stared at the water, he could hear groaning, as if someone were waking from a deep sleep. It seemed to be coming from under his boots and when he looked down, he could see that the heather was moving.

Before Jack could understand what was happening, the ground beneath him split open and a hand burst forth and clutched his ankle. His heart tightened as though the hand's grip had wrapped round it too. Instinctively he rammed his boot down onto the hand and twisted his heel. The hand instantly released him and he fled towards the doorway.

"Stop!"

Jack ignored the cry and sped on. He had almost hit the wall of water and was about to break its surface when the voice yelled out.

"Please!"

On hearing the voice again, he shot a glance back over his shoulder. He went no further instead he stood enthralled as the white heather on the walls drew back into the centre of the room and rose up, swirling into the air, moving faster with every twist until Jack could make out the figure of a woman. She held a heather shawl tightly round her shoulders and her robes beneath flowed onto the damp cobble floor. Three whorls of oak leaves held her white hair in place, framing her delicate ashen face.

"You're the Third Sister of the Heather," stammered Jack.

"Yes. I am Erica Cinerea," she said, her lips remained closed. She spoke directly to Jack's mind. "But how could you possibly know of me or my sisters for that matter?"

"They helped me find my way here… wherever here is," said Jack who by now had no intentions of fleeing and was instead walking towards her.

"They must have trusted you little one. But not even they could have led you beyond the Orb."

"They helped. The rest was an accident," explained Jack.

"An accident?"

"I fell in…. beyond the wall that is."

"That's not possible."

"What…" said Jack somewhat annoyed about being doubted. "Well, how did you get in then?"

"I do not know. But I did not enter alone."

Erica Cinerea stepped to one side and there in the corner, shrouded in a frosty silver mist stood a young girl. She wore a cream dress with a pink ribbon around her waist. Her face was pale as though lifeless. Jack noticed that around her neck hung a fine silver chain with a tiny glass jar dangling from it. He recognised it immediately. It was the same glass jar as the ones on the spiral staircase back in the Curraghard Tree.

"This is Grace."

"Hello Grace," said Jack.

"She cannot hear you. I hid her in this place nearly a hundred years ago. She was the last one I hid but I stayed to protect them all," said Erica Cinerea.

"You mean she's dead?" said Jack horrified.

"Oh no, she is very much alive." Erica opened her hand and a glass-like insect crawled across her palm. "This is a Spicicle; a Spider of Ice and it has kept Grace frozen in time. Every year on the 30th day in the month of July, the day of her birth, the Spicicle bites her. It keeps her from waking but the very moment it sinks its teeth into her flesh she is aware, just for an instant, of what has happened to her and every time she sheds a single tear. Over the years those tears have gathered and made a small pool at her feet but they too are frozen."

Jack approached the young girl.
"What age is she?"
"She told me she was born in the year 1757."
"You mean…" Jack calculated as quickly as he could, "… she's ninety!"
"No. She is only seven. That is the age she was when the Spicicle first bit her and that is the age she remains. It is time that has passed her by."

"But why would you do this to her?"

"To keep her safe, safe from the…." Erica's expression changed, as though confused and Jack could hear her again in his thoughts, stumbling for words.

"There… there….there was so many of them that day…. snatching and grabbing…. ripping and tearing at the hillside."

"Tearing at what?" shouted Jack.

"…A mist had fallen but we marched onward. No one would listen to me. Bad enough, there were thirteen of us in the group but to head on through the mist…just to get dandelion clocks for the girl back at the Curraghard tree."

"Dandelion clocks? But what happened?"

"Shimnavore…....." Erica screamed out across Jack's mind. "The Shimnavore….they were tearing at the clocks on the hillside, tearing them, snatching them ….grabbing them…. They caught the leader of our group….and what they did to him, such….such…a gentle creature… I cannot repeat….it is too… "

Jack could hear her labored breathing in his mind and he placed his hand upon hers. It felt damp and when he looked upon it, he could see a green stain. He realised she was injured. It had been where he'd stood on her.

"I'm so sorry." Jack interrupted. He took a handkerchief from his pocket and wrapped it around the wound."

"You were not to know."

Jack's act of kindness calmed her and she continued.

"When we saw what the Shimnavore were capable of we panicked. We ran away blindly in the mist and the last thing any of us could remember was falling. The rest is a blur. When we came to, we were on the other side of the Orb with no means of escape."

"The same thing happened to me, the falling bit that is. But I don't understand…. what do you mean 'we all?' " said Jack.

"There were originally to be fifteen of us in the group but Grace's sister injured her leg having fallen from her hammock, and all because someone thought it funny to remove the mattress beneath her."

"What!" said Jack in great surprise. He remembered what Cobs had told him when they first met. "Who were the others with you?"

"Grace's older sister had made a wish on a dandelion. She wanted to see her sister fly then for the two of them to meet who ever it was that granted the wish. So they entered the Kingdom of Mourne and met a family of Dandelion hunters. They were so excited they begged to go on a hunt with them. But when Grace's sister got injured she could not come."

"You mean Grace went hunting with the Family Hawksbeard."

"Yes…. But how could you know the Hawksbeard name?"

"I am travelling with the last of them."

"You mean Cobs?"

"Yes!"

As Jack spoke, he walked up to the young girl and touched her face. He looked into her frozen blue eyes and an ache so deep rose from within him. A tear welled up in his eye then rolled down his cheek and fell from his chin. It landed on the frozen pool of tears at Grace's feet and the moment it struck it began to sparkle. The pool glowed from within, becoming brighter and brighter until the icy surface cracked.

Chapter 26
Raise an Army

Jack watched as the frosted pool of tears dissolved and with it the silver mist that surrounded Grace. A warm rush of air on the back of his head made him turn round quickly. The heat was coming from Erica Cinerea. Her robes had turned from white to a reddish purple and their brilliant hues lit up the room. Jack could see that she was blushing with joy.

Grace began to stir from her hundred-year slumber. The frozen glaze that covered her eyes began to melt and Jack could see they were watery blue. For a brief moment he thought she looked strangely familiar.

"Can you hear me Grace?" asked Erica.

"Is it time again?" whispered the child.

"No Grace. The Spicicle will never be needed again. The one I promised, the one who holds the secret has finally come."

"We can leave?" asked Grace, her voice low but full of hope.

"Soon, my child."

Erica took Jack's hand. "It is said that the eyes are the windows to the soul. If that is true then your teardrop was the key that opened that window and returned Grace to me."

Jack looked down to the pool of teardrops at Grace's feet. Oh how they sparkled, like sunlight on morning dew.

He stooped and was about to put the tip of his finger on the tears but he withdrew his hand suddenly as though he'd been stung.

"These tears hold a magic too powerful to hold Jack. They can never be touched."

Erica removed the necklace from Grace's neck and handed it to Jack.

"Open the jar and fill it."

Jack knelt down by the tiny pool and placed the jar beside it. He removed the tiny cork stopper and holding onto the silver chain, dipped the bottle into the tears. Once it was full, he removed it and then placed the cork back in place, careful not to touch any of the tears on the outside of the jar.

He tried to stand but the weight of a cold hand pressed down upon his shoulder. Jack glanced up and he met Grace's stare. It was as if she was looking right through him like he wasn't there. A chill ran down his spine and a familiar fear gripped him.

Grace's hand moved from his shoulder and on to his face where she began to trace its contours. She closed Jack's eyelids and in that instant he saw a blinding flash of light. The century of time that had captured Grace began to play out in his mind. He could feel the multiple bites of the Spicicle and he began to understand the fear of never waking. He couldn't cope with all the emotions that Grace held inside her and he staggered but Erica steadied him before he fell.

"Thank you," said Jack holding out the necklace to Erica. She took it from him.

"Now you know what she has been through Jack. But you must go now."

"Aren't you coming too?"

"Soon Jack. We must stay until the effects of the Spicicle wear off. Grace is blind you see, but her sight will return. However, it will take a while so you must go on ahead of us. I will lead her and the others out in good time."

"Others!"

"Oh yes. All the Family Hawksbeard is here."

"Cobs' family is here?"

"Yes. We all fled the Shimnavore that day we were hunting the dandelion clocks. They will all wake up now but you have to go on alone."

Erica led Jack to a large circular stone in the centre of the room.

"Stand here."

Jack stepped onto a raised platform and Erica leaned down and placed the necklace over his head. The glass jar rested on his chest but it quickly began to heat up until it was too hot to bear. It seared into his skin forcing him to grab it in his hand. As soon as he held it, he could hear whispers coming from within the jar as though the waters inside were trying to talk to him.

He began to feel a little dizzy so he closed his eyes. Now all he could feel was the sensation of getting lighter, like floating high into the air. When he looked down, he could see all of the Mournes, from the Cloc Mor stone to Tollymore Forest, from his cottage in Annalong all the way to Fofanny Dam. All the Realms were below him and they were beautiful. He could hear the rushing winds in his ears and taste the icy waters from the mountain streams. He felt damp grass beneath his feet and the smell of every living creature and plant that dwelled there. He watched a full moon rise on the horizon and cast its silver shadow over the lands but suddenly the sights before him began to change. The clear water of the rivers and lakes turned blood red then the green hills fractured, swallowed by waves of molten lava. Everything burned.

Jack opened his eyes with a start. He was back on the circular rock in the centre of the chamber.

"What on earth was that?" he yelled.

"You have had a vision Jack. A premonition of your own. The tears within the jar have let you witness the second Holocene."

"But this can't happen," shouted Jack, "I won't let it."

"Only you have the power to stop it Jack," said Erica. "But you must swear to me that you will not tell Cobs of anything you've seen here. You must both continue on your MourneQuest, for you have yet to find the true secret of the Silver Orb."

Before Jack could ask what she meant the rock he stood upon juddered and a sound like grinding stone cogs echoed through out the chamber. Jack was about to jump off it but Erica ordered him to stay where he was.

The rock turned in an anti-clockwise direction and with each revolution, Jack rose higher as if he was standing on a giant screw being removed from a plank of wood. As he ascended, he had a bird's eye view.

He could see that the room's circular floor was carved into ten pieces and each slice had an Ogham symbol at the edge. Suddenly, something hit his head, forcing him to look up.

Large chunks of the ceiling were crumbling and falling. There was dust everywhere. Through half closed eyes Jack could see a symbol of three fish carved in stone fast approaching. He wanted to jump off the column but now that it was nearly two hundred feet from the ground, it didn't seem like a good idea. To his astonishment, the stone-fish on the ceiling began to move, they weaved in and out of each other, dipping and swirling. They had sprung to life. Their motion sent thunderous shocks through the room. Jack crouched down, his heart racing and threw his hands over his head trying to protect himself.

At the edge of the Assembly Pillar Cobs and the Dullahan stood staring into the water.

"The boy is lost," said the Dullahan.

"The waters would never keep him. He *will* return," replied Cobs emphatically.

A huge explosion hushed the both of them. They turned and looked towards the throne. It had fallen backwards to the ground and on the base they could see the symbol of three fish. From the hole left in the floor, they watched as Jack rose up and came to a stop. The base of the throne had been the ceiling of the hidden chamber.

Cobs ran to Jack, a broad smile across his face and he leapt up and hugged him tightly.

"Jack, my young man. I knew you'd come back but I did not expect so grand an entrance."

Jack hugged him back and he whispered into his ear. "I can't explain everything now Cobs but you have to trust me. I know what we have to do."

Cobs instantly noticed a change in Jack's tone. "Something's happened to you, hasn't it Jack? I can tell." Cobs leaned back a fraction. "There's a fear in your eyes that wasn't there before?"

"You have toppled my throne," said the Dullahan. "I hope you know what this means."

"No I don't," Jack replied.

"You are now the Leader of this Forgotten City but there is just one thing. Are you prepared to lead it?"

Jack inhaled deeply, his chest rising. He held his breath and paused looking down at the necklace resting around his neck.

"I do not want to command your people. I leave that to you," Jack replied. "I've only one thing I want you to do for me."

He made his request and the Dullahan bowed then left. Cobs and Jack were alone.

"I am about to face the greatest challenge of my life Cobs and I am so glad you are here to help me," said Jack resting his hands on Cobs' shoulders.

"I've never heard you speak like this before."

"A lot has happened since I stepped off this Pillar. I've seen a century in a single glance and I've been witness to the end of all the realms."

Cobs could not understand what the boy was saying but the newfound wisdom made him extremely nervous.

The sound of a door slamming interrupted them. The Dullahan had returned. It walked right up to Jack.
"Hold out your hand boy."
He placed something onto Jack's open palm.
"But..." Jack couldn't believe his eyes.
"But what?"
"My boat. You fixed it. The mast is back in one piece."
"Is it? I am sure I have no clue how that happened. I found it when I went to ask the City Crier to call for another assembly, as you requested. Everyone will be here soon."

Jack held the boat up in his hand. He could smell the oak and linseed oil. He closed one eye, squinted the other, and imagined the small boat sailing next to his fathers just like the morning before his eleventh birthday. The thought of his father made that familiar ache rise up inside him.

The Iron doors of the great chamber flung open and the creatures of the city flocked in. They took their places as they had done so many times before.

The Dullahan spoke. "I know I said the next assembly would not be for some time but all that has changed now. This assembly may be our last and because of this I want you to hear the words of someone not of this realm."

"Not of this realm," were the collective shouts of all those present.

"This child is not of this Realm," said the Dullahan sweeping back his long cloak to reveal Jack who was huddled close to Cobs.

The crowd hissed and jeered at them. The Banshees took flight and their ghostly forms swarmed above Jack's head.

"Cease," shouted the Dullahan. "You will hear what this boy has to say and any more outbursts you will deal with me." A lashing crack followed his voice and Jack could see the Dullahan holding a whip that looked as if it were made from a corpse's spine. He gulped hard.

The room fell silent and Jack took a small step forward. He looked at everyone gathered and his mouth grew dry but he fought the fear he held inside for he knew this was his true purpose and that thought gave him an inner strength.

"My name is Jack Turner and I am from the Outer Realm. I have come to warn you that I have seen what will happen to your lands. Your Inner Realm will collapse and you will all die but do not worry for the Mournes themselves will no longer exist!"

A wave of unrest rushed through the chamber.

Jack continued. "There is a battle to be fought, but not one of clashing steel from swords held aloft or cries of hatred from the mouths of the vengeful. This is a battle to be fought on wits alone."

The sounds became unbearable as all those gathered argued amongst themselves. One of them, a creature covered from head to foot in thick layers of matted hair and lizard-like scales stood up and shouted.

"Why should I join you? You mean nothing to me and the place you come from means even less."

"Here, here," came the shouts of a Merrow who pelted Jack with a rotten apple. The rest of the gathered crowd laughed as it hit him on the side of his face.

Jack just wiped his cheek, but all the while an anger was beginning to take hold of him. The jar of tears that rested began to heat up and within a few seconds they were burning hot. Jack placed his hand around the jar and closed his eyes. A voice from deep down inside him filled the chamber. He looked to the Merrow and said.

"You, more than most, want an end to this misery. To reach the end of the Devil's Coachroad."

The Merrow sat down in stunned surprise. "You cannot know that! No one knows that."

Jack looked back to the hairy lizard beast in the fourth row who had shouted out first. "And you, you are the one that has helped the Shimnavore most for you have slept through many a night-time watch."

The hairy beast quickly sat down.

"And as for you -" Jack pointed around the room to each creature sitting before him, his eyes still shut and he called out their innermost secrets.

"He cannot know these things!" shrieked a Banshee. Jack suddenly remembered the Family Tree in Pierce's castle and he realised that he'd gone too far. He was using his power to make people feel inferior and he felt terrible.

"I am sorry. I do not mean to bring shame upon any one here. I only mean to show you that your fears amount to nothing if you are not willing to join me. We have not a minute to lose for there is only one more full moon left and that is tonight. The Shimnavore will finish the cave then. It is probably in the InBetween as I speak."

Jack held up his two arms, his fists clenched and shouted," Who is with me?"

There was silence until there came a cry from a shadow high up in a corner of the chamber. "You have my following."

"And mine," came the shriek of a Changeling in the top row.

Several more voices joined in and by the time he had finished Jack had raised a grand army of eight. He looked at Cobs whose face was blank.

"This is futile Jack. We cannot defeat the Shimnavore with eight warriors," said Cobs.

"Eight! We can beat it with one as long as that one believes in himself. We have more than enough, now let's get ready."

The rows emptied fast and the mutterings reached Jack's ears as they brushed past him.

"It'll never work."
"Who does he think he is?"
"He'll be killed the second the Shimnavore sees him."
"What chance does he have?"
Jack listened as they passed him by, until he could listen no more.

"Get out all of you. You're cowards, afraid of change, afraid of what you do not understand."

The room emptied, all except for those who waited to hear Jack's plan. Jack spoke to each one individually.

The Dullahan knew its task, the Changeling his. The three Banshees didn't like their parts but they went along with it anyway. The Merrow and the Watershee quarreled over who did what but in the end they nodded in agreement.

The final creature, Jack noticed, stood with its knees knocking. Two bushy eyebrows met at the bridge of a tiny nose and its ears were set low on the sides of a head that twitched and flicked around at each change of sound within the room. It looked like a child but it wasn't a Changeling. It was a Sheerie. Jack whispered in its ear, "Are you alright?"

Now truth be told a Sheerie is known to have no power of speech. When it opens its mouth to utter a word it lets out a shriek so ear splitting it can turn a human mad but this was a Sheerie like no other. For a start, it was the offspring of a Land and Water Sheerie, a combination never thought possible and secondly it had been taught to speak by a motherly Banshee many moons ago.

"I'm just a bit nervous that's all. I only came down here because I saw the great wave go down the Bellmouth. I've never stepped foot in the city before and it's really scary," said the terrified Sheerie.

"Don't worry. I'm more afraid than you are but don't tell anyone," said Jack.

The Sheerie cackled. Jack had said exactly the right thing to put it at ease.

When each creature was told of their role in the battle, they stood up, even the Merrow shed her sealskin cloak in the depths of the pool then with new found legs stepped onto the land and joined the troupe.

"Get everything you need," shouted Jack. "We march tonight!

Chapter 27
Under the Mountain

By the first evening star, the small army had gathered at the city's gates. As Jack approached, they stood straight with eyes forward, chests out, and shoulders back, paying him the respect they knew he deserved. For never in the history of the Inner Realm had anyone shown such bravery. To face up to the Dullahan was one thing but to go after a Shimnavore was another.

In their hearts they knew they had little or no chance of returning alive, but two of the creatures, more than most knew they couldn't live any longer under the Shimnavore's tyranny. One of the Banshees had lost her daughter to the creature and the Changeling had his sister stolen away in front of his own eyes. Up until now they were helpless to prevent the deaths that followed. Instead they bided their time waiting for the day to be called to fight and now that day had come.

Jack walked along his ranks inspecting them. First, he crouched down to look at the eight inch high Watershee. He could see her innocent face, with chin held high, but he knew of her deadly beauty for Cobs had told him how she could devour a soul once she had lured them into the depths of a lake or pond. She was standing on her tiptoes trying to make herself look taller.

Next in line were the three Banshees, black as midnight and huddled so closely together that Jack thought they looked like a three-headed creature. They too were standing to attention but Jack smiled when he noticed they were in fact floating about a foot off the ground trying to impress him.

He gave a knowing nod to both the Sheerie and the Changeling and moved onto the Merrow who had taken to wearing her red-feathered cap but Jack explained to her that it stood out like a burning torch on a moonless night. She took it of immediately.

Finally, Jack came to the Dullahan. He looked up into the emptiness above its neck and gave a harsh stare. The Dullahan patted a leather glove on the spinal-handle of its whip that hung from a whip holster around a thick black belt. It bowed deeply.

Jack was checking their weapons or to be more exact he was checking to make sure they weren't carrying any for the most unusual thing about Jack's army was that not a single one of them carried a knife, a sword or an axe. Jack had forbidden it.

"No weapon had ever made a problem better before making it much worse." His father had said this to him many times when they talked about the history of Ireland.

"We will fight this battle in a way never fought before," Jack told them. "We need to get a move on. It's a long hike over Binnian Mountain, but remember, once we leave the city's gates and enter the Silent Valley we won't be able to hear each other, so if any of you have anything to say now's the time."

There was silence until the Sheerie coughed half as though to clear its throat and half as though to get attention.

Jack looked at it. "Do you want to say something?"

The Sheerie hung his head low. "It's just that... there's an easier way."

"Easier way!" the Banshees hissed in unison. "What do you know?"

The Dullahan stamped his boot into the gravel. "Let him speak."

"We don't have to go over the mountain," said the Sheerie trembling.

"What other way is there?" asked Jack.

"You see, the Shimnavore drove my race out of these hills and only for the kindness of the gentle Carricks there'd be no Sheerie left.

"Carricks!" shouted Jack, "I live not far from Carrick Little Mountain."

"That mountain was named after them," said the Sheerie, confident now he had Jack's attention. "They weren't just known as the Carricks though; we knew them by their true name, the Dunnywater Tunnelers."

"Tunnelers!" exclaimed Jack.

"Yes. There are tunnels running all through the Mournes. The main one runs right under Slieve Binnian all they way to Annalong Wood."

"Under Binnian mountain it is then," said Jack. "Let's go."

They left the Forgotten City and marched along the edge of the lake within clear view of the swirling Bellmouth. Jack tried not to look at it as he passed by for even the memory of falling down it still made him shiver with fright.

After a short distance, they came upon a low granite wall and the Sheerie hopped up onto it.

"There!" He mouthed, pointing to a stream that twisted down the hillside becoming a waterfall as it fell over a shelf of rock sending a fine spray into the air.

The small troupe watched as the Sheerie ran down a steep heather embankment towards the waterfall. It put one hand into the flowing water and tugged hard on something. Then a sound like the grinding of teeth came from behind the waterfall. The mist evaporated and the waters parted like curtains being drawn to reveal the mouth of a tunnel. The Sheerie beckoned everyone to come, ushering them inside as quickly as he could. The second the creatures crossed the threshold of the tunnel they could hear again.

"This doorway will close soon and the waterfall will hide it. Now we are in the tunnel we've no choice but to stay in it," said the Sheerie. "This door will stay closed until the one on the far side is opened."

"Alright," shouted Jack, "those who can see in the dark should go first."

Cobs and the Sheerie, whose eyesight was best suited to the task, took the decision to lead. Jack whose eyesight was the poorest went to the back of the group and the knowledge that there was no one behind him made him uneasy. He stretched out his hand and ran it along the side of the tunnel to help him feel a little more secure but the dank and weeping mould only made him more ill at ease. He began to sing a tune to keep his nerves at bay.

"As I roved by the dock side one evening so…"

He never got past the first line when Cobs shouted, "Hey Jack, how do you know that song? It's my favourite."

His voice echoed off the tunnel's walls.

"My Da always sang it but how'd you ever get to hear it?"

"A young girl taught me it, nearly a hundred years ago," came the reply.

The small troupe trudged on through the tunnel's putrid waters. Jack made his way, still holding his hand out, but noticed too late that part of the tunnel wall was missing. He fell sideways but iron bars that ran from the floor to the ceiling broke his fall.

"Ouch. What the heck are these?" said Jack quickly righting himself and rubbing his aching cheek.

"Prison bars Jack and beyond them lie the cells," said the Sheerie, "You wouldn't want to go in there and whatever you do don't look inside them."

"Why not?" said Jack.

"Just do as you're told Jack," shouted Cobs.

Jack walked on but the thought of being told not to do something made him want to do it all the more. He kept his hand held outward and at the sixth gap in the tunnel's wall, he knew he was at the sixth prison cell. At this point, he could resist temptation no longer and he had a quick peek but the sights he saw there terrified him. He walked on with a quick step wishing he'd done what he was told.

A surge of silver light greeted them when the door on the other side of the tunnel opened. A giant full moon sat on the back of Rocky Mountain making the night glow.

"We're at Annalong wood," said the Sheerie.

"Then up the valley is what we're looking for," said Jack.

They walked along the banks of the Annalong River until they were at the foothills of the Byshee Cave.

"We haven't long now. Get to your positions," commanded Jack.

Cobs looked up into Jack's eyes. "Are you sure you want to do this? Yours is the most dangerous task of all, but I promise I will do my best to see no harm comes to anyone here tonight."

"My wish is in that cave Cobs and I will make sure it comes true or I'll die trying."

"I won't let you down."

The troupe scattered and found their positions.

"Now we wait," said the Sheerie. "I hope this works,"

"I know it will," said Cobs crossing his fingers behind his back. "Oh and thanks for the rags to shove up my nose, they stink to high heaven but at least I can get closer now to the cave than I could've before.

Chapter 28
Battle Commences

Jack stood alone in the centre of the valley quivering with fear. There was no going back. He breathed in deeply trying to calm his nerves but instead of cool mountain air hitting his lungs he inhaled a mouthful of foul smelling gas. The familiar reek of burnt seaweed made him cough and he was instantly aware that the creature was near. He looked down the dark valley, from where the evil stench came from and he could see something prowling.

From its crouched position, next to the cave, the Sheerie shifted to get a better look down the valley but as he moved he dislodged large chunks of rock and sent them crashing down the hillside.

"Ahhhh... help! Someone help!" Jack screamed. He lay, where the rocks had come to rest, clutching his knee.

A hellish howl pierced the night sending a chill up Jack's spine and the silhouette of the biggest living creature he'd ever seen stepped out of the shadows.

Here it comes, thought Jack. *Nowhere to run now.*

The Shimnavore stood tall and its telescopic neck lengthened even further. A furrowed muzzle bore huge rows of raging fangs that snapped and snarled and great globules of slobber dripped from them as its head jerked from side to side.

Without warning the Shimnavore fell onto all fours, chest proud to the night sky, muzzle pressed to its ribcage and the eyes in the back of its head fixed on the direction of Jack's voice. It strode, backwards, on awkward joints that almost appeared to be dislocated, trampling the gorse under its mighty weight towards Jack.

"Now!" roared Jack.

The Banshees wailed and swooped down from their lofty heights, black hooded shrouds flapping like shadowy sails as they encircled the Shimnavore. Three ghostly-white faces spat and hissed at the beast, and with each pass, their fearsome screams grew.

On a rock near the cave the Merrow lifted a mass of sodden turf in her webbed fingers and pelted the Shimnavore with all her strength, cackling madly with every fistful of earth she flung.

From high in a tree, the Changeling stood on bowed legs and tried to straighten a crooked back. It put two gnarled hands to its thin-yellowed lips and let out a screeching caterwaul that forced everyone to cover their ears. It then bombarded the Shimnavore with spiked hawthorn branches snatched from a nearby tree.

A cacophony of sounds from Jack's small army filled the night.

The Shimnavore rose high on its haunches again, eyes darting like flies, searching for the culprits. When it spied Jack huddling on the ground clutching his injured leg its muscles coiled as it kicked up great clumps of earth, stampeding backwards towards its target.

Jack watched terror-stricken as the hulking mass sped towards him. He fought to get the words out and every second he hesitated the beast covered great swathes of ground. At the last second, he managed to shout.

"NOW!"

The Shimnavore hurtled on, ignoring a large grassy mound on its left flank, lurching towards its prey. The Dullahan saw his chance and flung off Jack's cloak. The lining, with its forty shades of green had blended into the mountainside, perfectly camouflaging him, making him almost invisible. He leapt up from his crouched position and yanked on his spinal whip. The rope attached to it strained and the noose, hidden in the dirt sprang up and snared the Shimnavore's hind leg. Without a moment's hesitation the Dullahan lifted the spine above his shoulders and plunged it deep into the ground like a spike but the Shimnavore careered onward towards Jack unaware of what had happened.

Jack forced himself to keep his eyes open, staring at the huge jaws, waiting for them to bear down on him but suddenly within an inch of his face, the Shimnavore jolted backwards. The rope around its leg jerked and the Shimnavore knew instantly it was trapped.

In a frenzied panic, the beast thrashed out, struggling to break free of its bindings. It clutched at the rope becoming more and more enraged with each failed attempt to free itself.

"We've caught it," shouted Cobs, hopping about gleefully.

The rest of the troupe gathered round the Shimnavore, just close enough to stay at rope's length.

"Your plan worked," said Cobs. "You were brave to use yourself as bait. The falling rocks were a great idea Jack, to lure the Shimnavore out, but using your cloak to hide the Dullahan was a stroke of genius."

"You were right Jack, a triumph of brains over brawn," added the Dullahan.

"I told you the Silver Bearded Drewron's rope would hold, didn't I?" said Cobs, trying to soak up some of the glory.

On hearing Cobs mention the Drewron's name the Shimnavore broke its gaze with Jack. It looked down at its hind leg and Jack swore he could see a hungered grin on its face. The Shimnavore's trident tail lashed out and with a single swipe severed the rope that bound it.

It got up high on its hind legs and loomed over everyone; flexing its forearms. It pulled two clenched fists together and the muscles across its chest hardened making its ribs crack. Then it let out a growl, so loud that the ground shook.

Everyone fled.
Everyone, except Jack.

The Shimnavore took one pace forward and Jack took one pace back. As the beast drew closer to the cave Jack could see its clasped fist grow brighter for he knew that inside its grasp were the last of the dandelion clocks. Jack's gaze went from the Shimnavore's claws, up the length of its sinewy arm, past its sturdy shoulder until he arrived at its eyes.

Jack stared at it but the Shimnavore just stared through him. There was something in its eyes but Jack could not figure out what.

Every time the Shimnavore moved Jack mirrored its actions for he didn't know what else to do. Like Cobs, he'd thought the rope unbreakable and hadn't expected to be standing one on one with the creature.

The Shimnvore's nostrils twitched and its head lowered. The eyes in the back of its head glared through hair that thrashed about as though caught in a vicious wind even though the night air was still. The beast opened an empty fist and pressed it into the earth then removed it. Both Jack and the Shimnavore looked down to the paw print and paused for a moment. They both looked up until their eyes met again.

This time the Shimnavore's gaze was unflinching. A thick blackened tongue slipped over its fangs and with a grating roar, it lunged into the air, towards the night sky, giant ribcage expanding. Its massive frame out-stretched as it twisted and turned in midair before two powerful legs dug back into the earth. Jack stood defenseless, scared beyond belief as the beast thundered towards him.

Instinctively Jack turned to run but he twisted his ankle and he fell just avoiding the grasping talons of the Shimnavore as it flew past him. As Jack lay on the ground, he caught a good look into the Shimnavore's eyes that bulged in the back of its head. He suddenly saw what was hiding in the creature's stare and in that instant; everything around him seemed to stop. He felt the jar around his neck becoming hot and he could hear the waters inside calling out to him but the voices were clear now. This time he fully understood what they were saying to him.

The daze left him as quickly as it had come and Jack watched as the Shimnavore continued to career onwards, struggling desperately to stop its hulking mass. After another ten steps, it tore into the ground and halted for a split second, and then it spun around for a return attack.

Jack tried to ignore the pain in his ankle as he stood up and fought to stay calm even though the Shimnavore was charging at him again. He watched every footfall of its approach with great care. It let out a thunderous roar just as it swiped at Jack's face. Jack took a single side step and clutched the chain around his neck. He tore it off and flung it with all his strength. He watched as the silver necklace glistened in the rays of the moonlight before the tiny jar that hung from it hit the back of the Shimnavore's head. The fragile glass shattered and the tears captured within exploded into its eyes.

Its body may have been impenetrable but Jack now knew its weakness. He saw that its eyes held no fear. They held nothing. The creature had no windows to its soul for it had no soul.

The Shimnavore's claws tore at the back of its head as splinters of blinding white light shot out from its eyes. Inside the Shimnavore's armoured skin, bones turned white hot and cold blood boiled. Molten fluid seared along scorched arteries and veins, burning its lungs, before incinerating its huge heart. An agonizing shriek ripped from the Shimnavore's throat and its long neck extended backwards then snapped.

It fell to the ground.

Dead.

Chapter 29

Loss of a Comrade

The troupe's joyous screams and laughter lifted into the night sky. The Changeling grabbed the Sheerie and hugged it. The Dullahan threw one of the Banshees high into the air then caught and squeezed her tightly. The other two looped the loop. The Merrow and Watershee locked arms and danced a jig. Cobs joined them in their victory but as he shouted out he noticed a voice was missing.

"Where's Jack?" he said in a panic.

The low hanging clouds parted, forcing the moon from its hiding place and its halo bathed the countryside in an eerie blue light. Cobs looked to the charred ground where the Shimnavore had fallen and there lying next to it lay a wizened old man with foam white hair. His breathing was shallow as though he was in pain.

Cobs scurried over to him, kneeled down, and looked deep into his eyes. They were the eyes of a little boy.

"Jack, you touched the Shimnavore!" said Cobs.

"Its tail caught me as it passed," said Jack faintly. "But...w-we did it...didn't we? Da will be home soon ...and Ma will be...so happy."

"Yes Jack, your wish is sure to come true," said Cobs placing his hand under Jack's head to comfort him.

"That's all I ever wanted...now I just want to sleep Cobs... please... just let me sleep."

Jack closed his eyes, his head fell to one side, and his breathing stopped.

Chapter 30
Hope Eternal

Jack lay lifeless, slain in the mud. The wrinkles on his face weren't as deep now and he seemed at peace. But his best friend was not about to give up on him.

"No!" Cobs roared. He grabbed Jack by the shoulders and shook him hard. "Jack, come back, come back!" But Jack did not move. He lay limp, blue-lipped, and silent.

Cobs knew he was gone and he gently lifted Jack's head placing it onto his lap. He rocked back and forth stoking his cheek, moaning in grief then he leaned in towards his ear and whispered, "It wasn't supposed to end like this. I'm so so sorry. I promised nothing would happen to you and I've let you down."

As Cobs held Jack close to him, he noticed a small flicker of light from a pocket in Jack's waistcoat.

"Quickly!" Cobs implored, "Everyone move, give me room!"

The creatures took a step backwards as Cobs frantically rifled through Jack's pocket.

"I've got it," he said, holding the obsidian stone in his hand. "Everyone turn your back on Jack and unless you want to go blind, don't look."

Cobs placed the stone on Jack's forehead and the instant it touched Jack's skin, the black stone dissolved and the thick vein of quartz crystal that ran through it flowed from its prison. It began to shine, growing brighter and brighter, engulfing Jack in a cocoon of azure blue light. His limp body rose from the ground and hung in the air as though suspended from invisible strings. The sound of a thousand choirs sang out then the light surrounding Jack began to grow dimmer then it shrank back on itself, shrivelling to the size of a match-head, before disappearing altogether. And there, on the grass lay a young boy.

Cobs ran to his side.

"Jack, Jack can you hear me. Are you alright?"

Jack's eyelids flickered for a moment, and then all of a sudden he sat bolt upright, opened his eyes wide, and gasped for air.

"You're back," shouted Cobs, "are you alright?"

Jack took short shallow gulps of air and slowly the blood returned to his cheeks.

"I'm fine Cobs." Jack whispered, "I've been granted the best wish of all."

"What was it?"

"I don't remember. All I know for sure is that he's safe," said Jack.

Jack placed his hand on Cobs' shoulder and pushed himself up.

"I've something I have to finish."

Even in his weakened state, Jack forced himself to walk over to the Shimnavore. He looked into the dead sockets that once held its eyes and with his thumb and index finger he closed its eyelids. Then with great care, he took the dandelion clocks from its claws.

Jack smiled as he trekked up the hillside towards the cave's entrance.

"What's he doing?" asked the Dullahan.

"I don't really know," replied Cobs, "but I'm sure he does."

Jack squeezed his way through the tight opening and crossed the two chambers until he arrived at the innermost cave. He stood in its centre and marvelled at the millions of tiny dandelion clocks. He knew the Shimnavore had been evil but they had created the most beautiful sight he had ever seen. Bright jewels of frozen light bounced off the walls radiating a stillness that both calmed and soothed him.

Jack could see where the cave's bare rock was still visible. He took each dandelion clock and with great care placed them into the small empty space and then he stood back, awestruck.

The clocks lining the cave were complete.

A sudden breeze blew up out of nowhere and ran through his hair toying with his curls. It tickled his neck and a tingle ran down his back. Jack had the same special feeling that he'd had in his bedroom the night he'd made his first dandelion wish.

Jack rolled his tongue,

Closed his eyes,

Roared his wish in his thoughts then blew as hard as he could.

His breath met the first clock and it trembled, rocking from side to side. Jack stared at it, holding his breath. After a few seconds it fell, toppling the clock next to it and it in turn, the next, like blades of grass falling in a summer breeze. Rows of clocks collapsed and a cascading avalanche swirled up in front of Jack. A snowstorm of clocks spun around him, moving faster, becoming a swirling tornado then in an instant, they raced out of the cave.

Jack ran to the entrance and he watched the trail of dandelions lift dragon-like into the night sky. They collided with the Orb and kaleidoscopic flashes of light burst outward. The dandelion clocks hammered the Orb's crystal skin demanding their release.

An arrow-like flare of molten colour ripped through the Orb as it cracked in two. Scarlet sparkles and silver squibs lit up the night and the Orb shattered, raining down on everyone below. The splinters of stain-glass colour hit their upturned faces and dissolved like winter snowflakes on warm skin.

Cobs felt a cold hand encircle his and he turned around expecting to see Jack. Instead, he stared into the eyes of his father. His heart lifted for the hurt he had carried inside him for so long disappeared and his disbelief turned to rapturous joy. His father picked him up and hugged him tightly. Cobs closed his eyes, trying to hold on to the moment, never wanting his father to let him go.

Cobs opened his eyes again and looked over his father's shoulder. He could see the rest of his family standing in a great arc next to Grace and Erica Cinerea.

He cried great tears as he jumped from his father's arms and sprinted to those of his mother. She squeezed him close to her as the rest of the family gathered around him. Jubilant screams and hollers of delight burst from Cobs as he looked into the eyes of his brothers and sisters.

"B..Bu…but how?"

"You have Jack to thank," he heard in his mind. The voice came from Erica Cinerea. Cobs turned and faced Jack.

"You, but how?"

"It doesn't matter now, does it? All that matters is that you have your family back. You are forgetting one thing though," said Jack.

"What's that?"

"The Orb is broken. It can't hold anyone prisoner in the Inner Realm. There is no Inner Realm anymore, only the InBetween and my Outer Realm."

Everyone cheered.

Cobs stood up on a rock and called for silence. He looked down on all those gathered below him. "The battle has been won, the Orb has been shattered, and I have been reunited with my family. I have Jack Turner to thank for all of this but I can never repay him." He jumped down from the rock and walked up to Jack with his hand outstretched. Jack could see the obsidian black stone with a thin vein of quartz running through its centre, sitting in his palm. He recognised it, but he knew the vein of quartz had been thicker when he last saw it.

"This is no ordinary stone," explained Cobs' father, "I gave it to Cobs a long time ago but even he didn't know where it originally came from. You see the Cloc Mor stone once held an immense power and the Elderfolk were able to channel it. With its help they built the Mourne Wall but the Shimnavore found out this precious secret and they planned to use it for evil. The Elderfolk were forced to drain the rock's power and open the Mourne Wall to enslave them."

"You mean the Holocene?" said Jack.

"Yes. The power unleashed from the stone allowed the wall to open long enough to capture the Shimnavore but in doing so nearly all the Elderfolk were killed. The family Hawksbeard was entrusted with the remaining power when the last of the Elderfolk died. They placed that power into the lighthouse in the Curraghard Tree, into all the dandelions that have grown since and into this stone."

Poitin gave the stone to Jack.

"But I can't accept this."
"You have no choice Jack. Now take it."
Jack put the stone back into his pocket.

The Dullahan surveyed the hillside and then spoke. "It will not be long before everyone knows the name of Jack Turner. He is the bringer of freedom to all the creatures cast into this realm and forgotten. They will soon roam again through the True Kingdom of Mourne and once again feel the rivers and streams on their skin. We are forever in your debt."

He approached Jack, knelt down on one knee, and whispered into his ear. Jack looked surprised.

"That's not possible."
"It is," replied the Dullahan.
The horde of night creatures left the hillside and travelled back towards the tunnel making their way back to the Valley of Silence.

"Let's get home Cobs."

The return journey to the Curraghard Tree is nearly a story in itself but by sunrise, they had arrived.

"Come in Jack, there is much to talk about," said Poitin.

"Thank you but I think I had better be off, if you don't mind. Someone is waiting for me."

Cobs led Jack down by the sugar-scented azalea, across the thirteen stepping-stones on the river Shimna, to the ruins of the old house.

"This isn't goodbye you know Cobs, I'll see you on my next birthday?"

"I'm sure of that. I cannot thank you enough for what you've given back to me."

"No. It's me that's grateful. I've been given the best gift of all."

The two friends hugged and Jack turned, kneeled down, placed his open palms on the mossy rocks, and closed his eyes. When he opened them again he was kneeling outside his cottage in Annalong holding the corner stone of the archway.

He ran to the front door and dashed to his Nanna Tess's room.

"Nanna Tess, Nanna Tess. You won't believe what's happened."

Tess pushed her hands onto the straw mattress and lifted herself up in the bed.

"Before you tell me any stories, have you got something for me?"

Jack hopped up beside her and planted a kiss on her wrinkled cheek.

"There."

"That's lovely Jack, but it's not what I meant."

"No?"

"No. I was wondering if you have something belonging to me. Something I gave you on the cliff."

"Cliff?"

"Yes you took my hopscotch stone but you never gave it back."

"What… That was you. You mean…."

"Yes Jack. Cobs gave me that stone nearly a hundred years ago. I fell from the hammock you see and I couldn't go on the dandelion hunt with the others. It was his way of making things up to me. It wasn't his fault what happened, no more than…" she stopped, "well you know."

Jack gave Nanna Tess the stone and she held it aloft. The summer sun shone through its quartz vein and projected an image onto the wall. Jack could see the Curraghard tree and the Hawksbeard family around its door.

"I watched your journey Jack and it was only when I saw the Rare Ring Ouzel fly over the wall that I knew I had to help you. Once you entered the Orb I couldn't follow you but I knew no harm could come to you once you had the stone."

"You could have warned me. "

"No Jack I couldn't, it was your journey. There is something else something else you must know."

"What's that Nanna?"

"The secret wasn't the hole in the Orb Jack."

"What?"

"Oh no Jack. You remember I told you that you were from a long line of stone masons,"

Tess pushed herself further up the bed.

"What I should have told you is that you were from the longest line of stone masons. You are the last of the Elderfolk. You were the secret all along. Only you had the power to break the Orb."

"Me!"

"Yes you. I was with Cobs when he found the book. I was the one who tripped him up and made him fall against the panel in the bureau. When I saw the book's cover I instantly recognised our family crest on it. You've never seen the crest but it shows three fish intertwined. I carved it into the boat your Da gave you for good luck. Cobs showed me the inside of the book and although we couldn't read it, I didn't need to.

"What do you mean you didn't need to?"

"The book spoke to me. The words that were written on the page I couldn't understand but the words in my head made sense. I even told Cobs what was written inside. There was one thing though, I never told him that I turned to the last page when he wasn't looking. That is when I knew."

"Knew what?"

"That when a mason's descendent was born on a day of equal light and darkness, that they would be the holder a great secret and that secret would be more powerful than all the dandelion wishes put together."

"That's what the Dullahan whispered to me but I didn't understand what he meant."

"Well now you do. You have great blood in your veins and I am proud to call you my grandson. Now go on with you. There's someone waiting for you at the pier."

Jack kissed her again and looked at her. This time when she smiled at him, her watery blue eyes did too. He hugged her tightly.

"See you later Nanna."

"Just in case I don't, I hope you have a great birthday and Jack, don't forget your dandelion wish," she whispered.

Jack was sure he'd misheard her but didn't ask her to repeat herself, instead he kissed her gently on her cheek, then ran out the door into the garden and through the gate that crashed against the wall. He glanced back at it, with disbelief and sprinted on down the hill.

Tess lifted the stone to her heart and felt the rise and fall of her chest next to her fist. A tapping on the open windowpane caught her ear and she looked to it. Standing outside was a young girl, no older than seven years of age. She called out. "Tess."

With a smile, Tess replied, "Grace, you've come back. I've waited such a long time for you. I am so sorry. I've been looking for you all my life and now you've found me."

"It wasn't your fault Tess, now come on, I haven't long here, now hurry."

Tess lay on the bed and placed the obsidian stone on her forehead. An azure blue light covered her, and a small choir sang out, before the light dimmed and the quartz inside the stone disappeared.

From outside, two young girls, one in a cream dress with a pink ribbon round the middle and the other in a red dress looked in through the bedroom windrow at the old woman. She seemed to be asleep and a pure obsidian black stone rested on her forehead.

"The quartz is all gone," said the girl in red.

"Yes Tess it is. It takes a lot of power to do what you just did. You look peaceful in there. Now let's go."

The two girls took each other by the hand and began to giggle. They were still giggling as they reached the bottom of Carrick little Mountain. With every step beyond the mountain, they began to fade until finally they were gone.

Down on the pier, Jack's mother stood alone. He ran up to her, and tugged on her apron. She smiled down upon him, and took him by the hand.

"Happy birthday Jack."

Together they looked out onto the horizon where the golden sun reflected silver off the water.

They waited…